THE RUSSIAN'S
ULTIMATUM

THE RUSSIAN'S ULTIMATUM

BY

MICHELLE SMART

First published in Great Britain 2015
by Mills & Boon, an imprint of Harlequin (UK) Limited,
Large Print edition 2015
Eton House, 18-24 Paradise Road,
Richmond, Surrey, TW9 1SR

© 2015 Michelle Smart

ISBN: 978-0-263-25629-1

Printed and bound in Great Britain
by CPI Antony Rowe, Chippenham, Wiltshire

This book is dedicated to my wonderful
parents and their equally wonderful spouses.
I love you all xxx

CHAPTER ONE

EMILY RICHARDSON DUCKED under the scaffolding over the entrance of the smart building in the heart of the city of London, strolled through the spacious atrium and headed to the wide staircase. When she reached the second floor she took an abrupt left, walked to the end of the corridor and pressed the button for the lift. Only once she had stepped inside and the door had slid shut did she allow herself to expel a breath.

Catching sight of her reflection in the mirrored wall, she raised an eyebrow. Power suits were really not her thing, especially ones dating back to the eighties. She felt suffocated—and her feet, in their patent black stilettos, were already killing her.

She had to fit in, she had to look as if she belonged in the building, so no one would give her a second glance. Her usual attire made her too noticeable—she would have been recognised be-

fore she'd got her foot over the threshold of the
building. Even with the suit, she'd have to be
careful. She'd timed her entrance to perfection—
not too early to be conspicuous but not so late
that the people she needed to avoid would be in
yet. So far, so good.

For this particular lift to work, a code had to
be punched in. She duly obliged and was carried all the way to the top floor and the private
offices held by the senior management team of
Bamber Cosmetics International—or, as it had
now been renamed, Virshilas LG.

The largest of the offices was held by Mr Virshilas himself. But not today; today Pascha Virshilas was in Milan.

Unlike in the rest of the building, renovation
work had yet to begin on the top floor. She imagined it wouldn't be long before it was remodelled
into Pascha Virshilas's idea of an executive suite
of offices.

She walked up the narrow corridor to an unas-
suming door that required a swipe card to open.
As luck would have it, Emily had such a card,
slipped from her father's wallet…

The door opened into a large, open-plan office.

It appeared empty and for that she expelled another breath of relief.

Holding her chin aloft and forcing her back straight, she walked through the central hub of the floor, gently swaying her empty black briefcase.

The place really was deserted. Excellent; she'd beaten the executive secretaries in.

It surprised her to find Mr Virshilas's office unlocked. Given how security-conscious the man was, she'd assumed it would be rigged with explosives in case an intruder made it through the security measures.

Maybe he wasn't as paranoid as she'd been told.

All the same, she paused after she'd opened it an inch, put her ear to the door and tapped on it. If the fates were conspiring against her and one of the cleaners was in there emptying his rubbish bin, she would apologise and say she was lost. She hadn't come this far to wimp out on a 'maybe'.

Her knock elicited no response.

She pushed the door open another inch, then

another. Heart racing, she entered the office, softly closing the door behind her.

She was in.

Time being of the essence, she scanned her surroundings quickly whilst reaching into the back pocket of her skirt and pulling out a state-of-the-art memory stick.

According to her source, Pascha Virshilas kept a laptop in all his worldwide offices. If her source continued to be correct, the laptop sitting on his desk was a centralised hub containing every file created by every department of every holding owned by Virshilas LG. This laptop contained the means of clearing her father's name.

Looking around, Emily could see that Pascha kept the neatest office in history. Not a single item looked to be out of place, not a single speck of dust or tiny crumb to be found. Even the intricate pencil drawings on the wall seemed to have been placed with military precision. All that lay on the highly polished ebony desk beneath the large window was the laptop and what looked to be a document file.

Flipping the laptop open, she pressed the button to switch it on. To her surprise, it fired up immediately.

Her eyebrows drew together. Had he forgotten to turn it off after his last use? From everything she knew about the man, this seemed out of character.

All the same, she wasn't about to look a gift horse in the mouth. For once it seemed the stars were aligning in her favour. The laptop being turned on had saved her an estimated two minutes' worth of hacking time.

Sticking the memory stick in the side portal, she pressed a few keys and the process began. Now all she had to do was wait.

If her hacking-whizz of a friend's estimates were correct, all the data contained within the laptop should be copied within six minutes.

The blue document file beside the laptop was a good inch thick. Emily opened the cover. The top sheet of paper had *Private & Confidential* stamped on it in angry red.

Pulling the thick sheathes of paper out of the file, she turned the top sheet over and began to read…

'Who the hell are you and what are you doing in my office?'

Emily froze. Literally. Her mind went blank, her brain filling with a cold mist. The sheets of paper held between her fingers fell back into place while her immobile hands hovered inches above the file.

Her gaze still resting on the papers before her, she forced her chin up to meet the stony glare of Pascha Virshilas.

Cold grey eyes narrowed. 'You,' he hissed, his chiselled features contorting.

She didn't know what was the greatest shock— that he'd caught her in the act, or that he recognised her. The one time she'd met him she'd looked completely different, so different she would have been hard pressed to recognise herself in the mirror.

With great effort, she forced her features to remain neutral. Now was not the moment to reveal her utter loathing of the man; she had to stay calm.

She'd met him six weeks ago at an event, optimistically billed as a party, thrown to celebrate the acquisition of Bamber Cosmetics by Virshilas LG and to allow the employees to meet their new boss. Emily had only attended as a favour to her father who, since her mother's recent death, became crippled with nerves at social events. Being a senior executive, his presence had been a requirement.

When she'd been forced to shake Pascha's hand, his only response had been a slight flicker of disdain before he'd looked through her and moved on to the next person. If he'd bothered to wait and talk to her, she could have apologised for her inappropriate attire and explained that she'd rushed over from work without having time to change. She'd been busy at a fashion show and it was mandatory for the designers of the house she worked for to dress the part.

Emily and her father had stayed at the party for a polite hour before making their escape.

She doubted her escape from Pascha's office would be as successful.

'I asked you a question, Miss Richardson. I suggest you answer it.'

'But you've just answered the question of who I am yourself,' she answered with more bravado than she felt. Her memory of Pascha Virshilas was vivid, yet in this office he appeared magnified. Impossibly tall and broad, even the crispness of his white shirt and impeccably pressed grey-striped trousers couldn't hide the muscularity of his physique. If anything, it enhanced it. And that face… Chiselled perfection a sculptor would struggle to replicate.

'Don't play games with me. What are you doing in my office?'

Her gaze flickered to the small stick poking out of the side of the laptop. From Pascha's vantage point, he would only be able to see the upright lid. He might not see the stick at all. If she was lucky, she might just be able to escape with the data.

Using all the nonchalance she could muster, Emily leaned forward so her chest rested on the desk. 'I was passing and thought I would pop in to see how you're settling in.' As she spoke, she inched her fingers forward, placed her knuckles either side of the memory stick and tugged it out, enfolding it into the fist of her hand.

If he saw what she'd done, he gave no visible sign.

She got to her feet and casually placed her hand

in her back pocket, releasing the stick into its tight confines. She had no choice but to brazen this out, whatever its conclusion may be. 'As I can see you've settled in fantastically, I shall leave you to it.'

'Not so fast. Before I let you go anywhere, empty your pockets.' Pascha's English was delivered with curt precision but with a definite trace of his Russian heritage in its inflection. Deep and rich with a hint of gravel, it sent the most peculiar tingle whispering over her skin.

'No chance,' she said, inching her way round his desk, slowly closing the gap between herself and the door to her side. She silently cursed herself for not paying more attention to the internal door Pascha had appeared through. She'd seen it when she'd first stolen into the office but had barely registered it; she certainly hadn't given it more than a cursory glance.

'I said empty your pockets.'

'No.' Her eyes darted to the door. She might be twenty-six but she'd been a nimble runner in her school days. She was half his size and figured she must be quicker than him...

It didn't surprise Pascha in the least when

Emily made a run for it, shooting to the door and tugging on the handle.

'It's locked,' he informed her calmly.

'I can see that,' she snapped.

'It won't open until I press the button to release the lock, and I won't do that until you give me what's in your pocket.'

Her pretty heart-shaped face glared at him, defiance pouring off her.

It was hardly surprising he hadn't recognised her from the camera that piped to a small screen in his private room. When he'd met her at his buy-out party, she'd been dressed in a long, black lace dress with ruffles, complemented by a pair of black biker boots and dark, dramatic make-up. All the black had contrasted sharply with her porcelain skin.

While the other women at the party had made an effort with their attire, Emily had deliberately set out to subvert. All she'd needed was a black veil sitting atop her long, dark ringlets which had spilled out in all directions and she'd have been the perfect gothic bride.

Today, though, she had tamed her curls into a bun—although tendrils were falling round her face—and was dressed in ordinary business attire of a knee-length navy skirt with a matching blazer and a delicate cream blouse. On her feet were ordinary, businesslike black court shoes and her face was make-up free. No wonder he hadn't recognised her, not until she'd raised those dark-brown eyes to meet his.

He would have recognised those eyes anywhere, dark but with flickers of yellow firing through them. Under the light of the function room the party had been hosted in, the colours had melded together, glimmering like a fire opal.

Those same eyes were staring at him now, loathing radiating from them.

He held his hand out and waited. If necessary, he would wait all day.

It wasn't necessary. Emily slipped her hand into her back pocket and pulled out a small silver device. She dropped it into the palm of his hand and stepped straight back, away from him.

As he'd suspected: a memory stick.

He strolled round to his seat, still warm from her bottom, and folded his arms. 'Sit down.'

After a beat, Emily grabbed the chair opposite

him and dragged it to the other side of his office, literally as far away from him as she could get it.

'So, Emily, it is time for you to start talking. Why were you trying to steal the files from my laptop?'

'Why do you think? I'm trying to prove my father's innocence.'

'By stealing my files?'

'I had to do *something*. According to my sources, you haven't even started the investigation into the missing money you've accused him of taking. The stress of it all is making him seriously ill.'

Emily would do anything in her power to clear her father's name. Anything. She had to give him something that would make his life—make *him*—feel as if it were worthwhile again.

As much as it pained her heart, Emily knew *she* would never be a good enough reason for her father to go on.

She'd watched him go through these dark times as a child, long periods where he wouldn't get out of bed for weeks on end. It had been terrifying. Back then, her mother had held them all together:

had held *him* together. But now her mother was dead. The rock they'd all relied upon was gone.

In the space of three months her father had lost the wife he'd adored and been suspended from the job he'd taken such pride in. The threat of the police knocking on his door and a subsequent prison sentence loomed over him. With hindsight, it had been obvious he would try to kill himself. He'd very nearly succeeded.

Losing her mother had been the single most devastating thing that had ever happened to her, a fresh, open wound that couldn't begin to heal while her father's mental and physical health were so precarious. If she were to lose him too…

Pascha gathered the file Emily had been reading when he'd caught her. So she had sources within his company, did she? That was something to think about later on. There was a much more important factor to consider first, namely how much of the file she'd read. He had no way of knowing how long she'd been in his office before he'd caught sight of her on the monitor. No longer than ten minutes, that was certain, as that had been the length of time since he'd left it. But long enough to read about things she had no business knowing.

'We will move on to the subject of your father shortly,' he said. 'In the meantime, tell me what you read in this file. And don't say you didn't rcad anything, because you were engrossed in it.'

For long moments she didn't answer, simply stared at him, her eyes squinting as if in thought. As if she were weighing him up… 'Not much. Only that a company called RG Holdings is buying out Plushenko's.'

Plushenko's was a Russian jewellery firm whose trinkets were regarded as some of the most luxurious in the world and came with a price tag to match, the Plushenko brand rivalling that of the other famous Russian jeweller, Fabergé. At least, it *had* been regarded as such. In recent years the jewels had lost much of their lustre and sales were a fraction of what they had been a decade ago. Amidst the highest secrecy, Pascha was gearing up for a buyout, using a front company.

'Oh, and I read that *you* own RG Holdings but that your name is being kept off all the official documents between RG and Plushenko's.' Her brow furrowed, as if she were trying to remember something, then her lips twisted into something resembling a smile. 'What was the phrase I read? Something along the lines of, "it is imperative that Marat Plushenko does not learn of Pascha Virshilas's involvement in this buyout". Was that it?'

Only with the greatest effort did Pascha keep his features still. Inside, his stomach lurched, his skin crawling as if a nest of spiders had been let loose in him.

Her brown eyes held his, as if in challenge, before her lips curved upwards—amazing lips, like a heart tugged out at the sides. Her eyes remained cold. She leaned forward. 'It's obvious this buy-out is important to you and you need to keep it a secret. I suggest we make a deal: if you agree to withdraw the threat of legal action towards my father, I will keep the details of the Plushenko deal to myself.'

Pascha's fingers tightened on the document in his grasp. 'You think you can blackmail me?'

She raised her shoulders in a sign of nonchalance. 'You may call it blackmail but I like to think of it as us making a deal. Clear my father's name. I want it in writing that you'll exonerate him from any potential charges or I will sing from the rooftops.'

Emily could see by the whitening of Pascha's knuckles that he was fighting to keep his composure.

How she kept her own composure, she did not know.

She'd never been a wallflower, not by any stretch of the imagination, but she'd never been one for making war before either. To stand up against this powerful man—a man capable of destroying her father; of destroying her too—and know she was winning… It was a heady feeling.

From despair and anger at getting caught and failing her father, she'd found a way to salvage the situation.

'I can have you arrested for this,' Pascha said, his voice low and menacing.

'Try it.' She allowed herself a smile. 'I'll be entitled to a phone call. I think I'll use it to contact the firm Shirokov—is that how you pronounce it?—and see if they'd be interested in representing me.'

How Pascha stopped his tongue rolling out the volley of expletives it wanted to say, he did not know.

Shirokov was the firm representing Marat Plushenko in the buy-out.

She dared to think she could threaten and blackmail him? This little pixie with a tongue as curling as her hair dared to think she could take him on and *win*?

He'd spent two years trying to make this deal happen, had even bought Bamber Cosmetics a few months ago as a decoy to avert any suspicion.

And now Emily Richardson had the power to blow it all to hell.

If Marat Plushenko heard so much as a whisper that Pascha was the face behind RG Holdings, he would abandon the deal without a backward glance and Plushenko's, the business the late, great Andrei Plushenko had built from nothing, would be ground to dust. His legacy would be gone.

And so would Pascha's last chance at redemption.

Could he trust her? That was the question.

He had no doubt her actions in stealing his files had been driven by exactly what she claimed—to prove her father's innocence. He almost admired her for it.

But beneath the collected exterior lurked a wildncss. It cchocd in the flickers of light emitting from her dark eyes. He could feel it.

This was a woman on the edge.

That, in itself, answered his question.

No, he could not trust her.

In exactly one week, the Plushenko deal would be finalised, the contracts signed. Seven whole days in which he would be wondering and worrying if she really was capable of keeping her mouth shut, if something innocuous could set her off to make a phone call to Marat's lawyer.

Beneath Emily's bohemian exterior, which even the plain suit she wore couldn't hide, lurked a sharp, inquisitive mind. A sharp mind on the edge could be a lethal combination.

An old English phrase came to mind: keep your friends close and your enemies closer.

This deal was everything. It *had* to happen.

It had been eight years since he'd walked out on his family. It was too late to make amends with the man who'd raised him as his own, but he could restore his legacy and, maybe then, finally, his mother would forgive him.

And for that reason he needed to make Emily disappear…

CHAPTER TWO

EMILY DID NOT like the thoughtful way Pascha appraised her, leaning back in his chair with his arms folded, his long legs stretched out beneath his desk, ankles crossed, handmade brogues gleaming.

She'd never seen such stillness. It was unnerving. Almost as unnerving as her attempt to blackmail him. But then, she'd never thought she would break into an office with the sole intention of stealing data from a billionaire's laptop.

After what felt like an age, where Emily's skin became tense enough to snap, Pascha leaned forward to rest his elbows on the desk and draw his fingers together.

'So, Miss Richardson, you think you can blackmail me to get what you want? I will not be threatened and I will not have the deal I've spent two years working on be destroyed.' The grey in his eyes glittered with loathing. 'I will not capitulate to your demands. No. *You*, Miss Richardson, are going to disappear.'

That made her sit up straight. She shook her head, as if unsure she'd heard him correctly. 'What? You're going to make me *disappear*?'

'Not in the sense you're thinking,' he said shortly, aggrieved to see her face had turned white. What kind of a man did she think he was? 'I can't take the risk of you disclosing the specifics of this deal, so I need you to disappear for a week.' And he knew the perfect place to take her.

Emily stared at him with wide, disbelieving eyes that held a hint of relief, probably at the confirmation he wasn't going to make her disappear via a wooden box. 'You can't be serious.'

'I am never anything but serious.'

'I don't doubt it. But I'm not going anywhere.'

'Yes, you are. I will agree to clear your father's name but in return you must agree to go into hiding for a week.'

He had to give her something in exchange, that much he knew. And, seeing as it was her father's name she wanted to clear, then that was what she would have. It was hardly a trivial sum either. One-hundred-and-fifty-thousand pounds had gone missing on her father's watch. He was the only person who could have taken it.

Her stomach roiling, Emily forced her mind to think clearly. As deftly as a professional tennis player, Pascha had regained control of the court. But this wasn't a game. Not to her. And, she knew, not to him either. What he was demanding of her was unbelievable, yet the set expression of those cool, grey eyes and the line of those wide, firm lips showed he wasn't bluffing. 'I can't just leave…I have commitments…'

'You didn't think of those commitments when you entered my office for illegal purposes.'

'Yes, I did, but I only planned on losing a couple of days if I got caught. Not that I expected *you* to catch me. I was told you were in Milan.'

'You really are remarkably well-informed.' Those gorgeous lips curved into the semblance of a smile. *Gorgeous lips? Had her anger addled her brain…?* 'But have no fear—I *will* learn who your mole is.'

She threw him a tight 'that's what you think' smile. Emily would never sell out a friend, especially to a man as dangerous as Pascha Virshilas, who ruined people's health and reputations for fun. She would bet that was the extent of any fun he had. He was so buttoned up, he probably even treated sex with the utmost precision.

And now she was imagining his sex life— where on earth had that come from? He'd unnerved her more than she'd credited.

Pascha rose to his feet and looked at his watch. 'I will give you five minutes to make your decision: your father's freedom in exchange for yours.'

'But where will I go? I have nowhere to go *to*.'

'I have somewhere to take you. It's safe and out of the way.'

Leaving her standing there to glower at his retreating figure, Pascha opened the inter-connecting door and stepped into his private space.

Emily would agree. Complying would give her exactly what she'd come here for.

He pulled out his phone and fired off an email to his PA, telling her to rearrange all his appointments for the next two days. As he wrote, he ruminated over the arrangements needed to get Emily out of the country and then immediately fired half a dozen more emails to the people and organisations he paid to make things like this happen.

Not that he'd ever done something quite like *this* before. And, if he felt any discomfort over what he was doing, he was quick to remind himself that she'd thrown the first ball. Emily had broken into his office to steal his company's data and then had tried to blackmail him. She didn't deserve him to feel any guilt.

Everything was in hand with regards to the Plushenko buyout. All the negotiations had been finalised; now it was just a case of dotting every 'i' and crossing every 't'. His lawyers were in the process of doing just that. There was nothing more for him to do other than sign the final contracts in exactly one week.

Escorting Emily to Aliana Island wouldn't affect anything. He could accompany her there and be back in Europe within thirty-six hours. And yet…

Pascha didn't like leaving anything to chance. He wanted to be there on the scene should any unexpected crises be thrown up, not halfway round the world with a blackmailing thief.

The inter-connecting door opened and Emily

burst into his private space, a space not even his executive secretary or PA were permitted to enter. More curls had sprung free from the bun she'd wedged her hair in, ebony tendrils falling over her face and down her back.

Without any preliminaries, she launched straight in. 'If I agree to effectively be kidnapped by you, I want it in writing that you'll exonerate my father from any and all charges.'

'I've already agreed to that.'

'I want your *written* guarantee. I doubt he'll ever be in a position to return to work, so I also want you to back-date the money he's been denied since being under suspension. And I want you to give him a decent pay-off of, say, a quarter of a million pounds.'

Pascha shock his head, almost laughing at her nerve. 'Your demands are ridiculous.'

She shrugged mutinously. 'That's what I want. If you agree to *my* demands, then I will agree to *your* demands.'

'I think you forget who is in the driving seat. I'm not the one whose father's future hangs in the balance.'

'True. But your wish for secrecy over your involvement in the Plushenko deal *is* in the balance.' Here, her face transformed, lighting up with faux sweetness. 'Either you agree to my demands or I whistle it to the world. We can call it a deal of mutual benefit or, if you prefer, mutually beneficial blackmail.'

Emily had never been on the receiving end of such pure loathing before. It radiated off him like a rippling wave.

She refused to cower.

She didn't care what the motivation was for his buy-out, knew only that it had to be something more than a simple business deal. Either that or the man was completely insane because no one went to such great lengths to secure a business deal.

No. For Pascha Virshilas, this buy-out was, for whatever reason, personal. And if he could use her emotions for leverage then she could certainly use his emotions for her own benefit—or, in this case, her father's.

Now the ball was back in his court.

After what felt like an age, he gave a sharp nod. 'I will agree to your demands with regards to your father, but you *will* disappear until my buy-out is complete. If at any point you find an opportunity to talk and are stupid enough to take it, our deal will be null and void and I will personally ruin the pair of you.'

Pascha pulled up outside the house in the London suburb Emily had given him as her address.

'You live here?' The cosy, mock-Tudor house was nothing like the home he'd imagined she would have. 'This is my father's home,' she answered shortly. 'I rented my flat out and moved back in a month ago.'

'That must have been a come-down, moving back in with your parents.'

She fixed him with a hard stare. 'Do not presume to know me or know anything about my life. Give me twenty minutes. I need to arrange some matters and get my stuff together.'

He opened his door before returning the stare. 'I'm coming in with you.'

'You certainly are not.'

'I'm not giving you a choice. Until we get to your destination, you're not leaving my sight.'

The fire running in her eyes sparked. 'To be

clear, if you say or do anything to upset my father then our agreement can go to hell.'

'Then you will be the one dealing with the consequences.'

'As will *you*.' Before his eyes, her face transformed, the hardness softening to become almost childlike. 'Please, Pascha. He's in a very bad place. You probably won't even see him but, if you do, please be kind.'

He'd never had any intention of upsetting her father. All the same, he found himself agreeing to her heartfelt plea. 'I will say nothing to upset him.'

And, just like that, she went back into her hard shell and jumped out of the car. 'Let's go in, then.'

He followed her through the front door and into a spacious yet homely house.

'Dad?' she called, shouting up the stairs. 'It's only me. I'll be up in a minute with a cup of tea for you.' Not waiting for an answer, she headed into a large kitchen-diner, put the kettle on and reached for the house phone.

Pascha grabbed her wrist before she could dial the number. 'Who are you calling?'

'My brother. I told you, I have things to organise. Now, take your hand off me.'

Not trusting her an inch, he complied, stepping back far enough to give them both a little space, but remaining close enough to disconnect the call should she try anything.

'James?' she said into the receiver. 'It's only me. Look, I'm sorry for the short notice, but I need you to come and stay with dad for the next week and not just tonight.'

From the way she sucked her angular cheekbones in, and the impatience of her tone as the conversation went back and forth, she wasn't happy with her brother's responses.

Emily was clearly a bossy big sister but beneath it all he heard genuine affection. He could well imagine her ordering her brother around from the moment of his birth.

His mind turned to the man he'd always regarded as a brother, the same man who would sooner drive Plushenko's—the business he'd inherited from their father—into the ground rather than sell it to Pascha.

While Pascha had openly hero-worshipped him, Marat had never made any secret of his loathing for Pascha. When Pascha had been seriously ill and death had been hovering, real, Marat had *wanted* him—the boy he'd liked to call the cuckoo in the nest—to die.

Emily's conversation ended with her saying, 'Mandy's around during the day if you need to go into the office. I'm only asking you to come for a week—you'll be fine. Amsterdam will still be there when you get back.'

She disconnected the call and immediately put the receiver back to her ear, dialling yet another number. This time, she relayed that an emergency had come up and asked whoever was on the receiving end to tell someone called Hugo that she needed to take a week's leave of absence.

'Are you done?' Pascha asked when she'd replaced the receiver.

'Yes.'

'No boyfriend to call?' He didn't even attempt to hide his sarcasm.

In response, she threw him the hardest look he'd ever been on the receiving end of, and in his thirty-four years that was saying something.

'No.' With that, she went back to the freshly boiled kettle.

'I take my coffee black with one sugar,' he informed her as she tossed a teabag into a mug, poured hot water onto it, followed by a splash of milk, and gave it a vigorous stir.

'That's nice.' She picked up the mug and swooped past him.

'It is good manners to offer guests refreshments.'

She came to an abrupt halt and spun around, somehow managing not to spill a single drop of tea. 'You are *not* a guest in this house and you never will be.'

For a moment, Pascha seriously contemplated forgetting his promise to send Emily somewhere safe and simply lock her in a sound-proof cupboard for a week.

Keeping close to her tail, he followed her up the stairs. When they reached the top, she turned back to him. This time she whispered, although she still perfectly managed to convey her hatred towards him. 'This is my father's room. Do not come in. Seeing you might just tip him over the edge.'

'Then keep the door open. I want to hear what you're saying.'

'You'll find our conversation scintillating.' She rapped her knuckles on the door, pushed it open and stepped over the threshold into a dusky bedroom, curtains drawn.

'Hi, Dad,' Emily said, speaking in such a gentle voice he could easily have believed it was someone else talking. 'I've made you a cup of tea.'

Pascha watched as she went to the window and drew the curtains back.

'Let's get some air in here,' she said in the same gentle voice, opening the window. 'It's a beautiful day. Honestly, Dad, you would love it out there. It really feels like autumn now.'

The daylight streaming into the room allowed Pascha to spot the full-length mirror on the wall, which gave him a perfect view of the still figure in the bed.

With Emily keeping up a stream of steady, gentle chatter, the figure slowly rolled over and lifted his head an inch before slumping back down.

Pascha's jaw dropped open to see him.

Malcolm Richardson was unrecognisable from the man he'd suspended just a month ago.

He looked as if he'd aged two decades.

A stab of something Pascha couldn't place jabbed in his guts.

It wasn't long before Emily re-joined him. 'Get a good look, did you?' she shot as she sidled past and over to a room on the other side of the landing.

'Don't be facetious,' he snapped, speaking through gritted teeth. 'When will your brother be here?'

She hadn't been exaggerating. Her father really was in a bad way.

'As soon as he finishes his meeting.'

'And he can care for your father?'

'Yes. He runs his own business—he's a financial advisor and sets his own schedule. The next-door neighbour pops in during the day when she can.'

'We need to make a move soon,' Pascha said, trying to ignore the new insistent jabbing in the pit of his stomach. However much his conscience might be turning on him, he couldn't let Emily stay. The risk was too great. 'We have a flight slot to fill.'

'You're taking me abroad?'

'Yes.'

'I expected you to leave me in a dungeon some-where.'

'That's a very tempting thought.'

She opened the door with a scowl. 'You can come in, but only because I don't want my dad finding you out here.'

Emily took a deep breath and admitted Pascha into her room.

He made no comment, just stood there taking it all in.

To her chagrin, she was embarrassed for him to see it. She'd done her best, but comparing it to the sterility of his office made her see all the flaws. It was as tidy and as organised as she'd been able to manage but it was hard cramming an entire life into a childhood bedroom.

She thought with longing of her cosy flat, could only hope her short-term tenants were treating it with respect.

She pushed the thought aside. It could be months before she was able to move back. Tortur-ing herself wouldn't change her circumstances.

'It's going to take me a while to get my things together,' she said, mentally shaking herself. 'Feel free to take a seat.'

'And where am I supposed to sit?' he asked. The small armchair in the corner was piled high with old clothes she planned to recycle into something new.

'On the floor?' she suggested with faux sweetness, yanking open the wardrobe door, glad she could hide her flaming cheeks.

Her room wasn't messy but it was filled with so much *stuff.* A lifetime's worth. If she didn't need to keep James's room free for the times he came to stay, she would appropriate it.

She would rather rip her own heart out than use her mother's small craft study. How many hours had they spent together in that room, working together, her mother teaching her how to create her own clothes? Too many to count.

Ignoring her suggestion, Pascha gathered the pile of clothes and placed it on the floor atop a neat stack of magazines, which promptly fell down under the weight. He raised an eyebrow then gingerly took a seat.

'Seeing as you're shunting me off abroad, what kind of weather should I pack for?'

'Hot.'

She pulled a face.

He leaned forwards slightly, resting his elbows on his thighs and exposing the tops of his golden forearms. 'You don't like the heat?'

'It makes my skin itch.' Disconcerted that a tiny glimpse of his *arms* made her blood feel thick and sluggish, she opened a drawer, gathered an armful of underwear and dumped it unceremoniously into the suitcase. Feeling Pascha's eyes watch her every move was even more disturbing, making her feel dishevelled and strangely hot.

Wanting to get out of the close confines of her bedroom as soon as possible, she packed quickly, throwing armfuls of garments into the case.

'I need to get changed,' she said, once she was satisfied she had enough suitable clothing for a week in the sun.

Pascha eyed her coolly before inclining his head and turning his chair so his back was to her.

In any other circumstance he would have left the room and given her the privacy she needed. In this circumstance, he could not.

He tried to tune out the sound of a zip being pulled down, the rustle of clothes being shed.

Determinedly, he focused his mind to running over the day's stock prices. Anything other than think about what was happening behind him where Emily was undressing…

He swallowed, trying to bring moisture into a mouth that had run dry.

He would not allow his thoughts to stray into such inappropriate territory.

Emily was leaving the country with him unwillingly, through circumstances neither of them could have wished for. That she was a single female should not mean anything.

All the same, the air trapped in his lungs didn't expel until she said, 'I'm decent.'

He twisted his chair back around.

She'd changed into a long, floating black dress with thin sleeves and was placing the business outfit she'd worn onto a coat hanger.

'So you *do* know to hang clothes properly,' he said as she hooked it into her wardrobe.

Her dark-brown eyes caught his and narrowed. 'These belonged to my mother. She did the occasional temping work.'

Belonged…? 'Your mother is…?'

'Dead. Yes.' The way her gaze fixed on him, it was as if she held him personally responsible for her loss. But there was something else there too, a flash of misery, quickly hidden but sharp for all its briefness.

'I'm sorry.' He truly meant it, too.

'So am I.' Her mouth set in a straight line that he understood to mean *this topic is not open for discussion,* Emily undid the bun holding the few tresses that had not already escaped before scooping the mass of curls back up and shoving a tortoiseshell comb high on the top, ringlets spilling over her face in a style that accentuated her high cheekbones.

'Is this really necessary?' he asked when she sat on the dressing table chair and began applying make-up.

'Yes,' she said, cleverly darkening her eyes. While she didn't go as far as she had at his party, there was more than a little hint of the theatrical when she'd finished.

He hated to admit it but the look really suited her.

He looked at his watch. 'If you're not ready in two minutes, I will carry you out of the house.'

'Good luck with that.'

Her stony gaze met his through the reflection in the mirror. For the briefest of moments, something sparked between them, a look that sent a wave of heat sailing through his skin and down to his loins.

Emily broke the look with an almost imperceptible frown.

'What's the weight limit for my luggage?' she asked, packing cosmetics into a large vanity case.

'We'll be travelling on my jet so there are no limits.'

'Good.' She dived back into her wardrobe.

'Now what are you getting?' His irritation had reached maximum peak, both at her attitude and the unfeasible reaction she seemed to be igniting within him.

The sooner he left her on Aliana Island, the better.

'My sewing machine.' She pulled out a large square case and dumped it on the bed beside the suitcase.

'Would you like me to un-plumb your kitchen sink for you while you're at it?'

The ghost of a smile curled on her cheeks, but she ignored his comment and slid under the bed.

Exasperated beyond belief, Pascha was suddenly distracted by the sight of dark-blue nail varnish on her pretty toes…and a small butterfly tattoo on her left ankle.

He couldn't say he liked tattoos but he couldn't deny that Emily's was tasteful. Delicate, even.

When she re-emerged, her hair having escaped the tortoiseshell clip and fallen down her back, she pulled out four large cardboard tubes.

'What's in those?'

'Fabric.' At his questioning look, she added, 'Well, it's pointless taking my sewing machine if I have nothing to make with it.'

'Have you got your passport?'

'It's in my handbag.'

Gritting his teeth, Pascha got to his feet and lifted the weighty suitcase. If he'd known she kept her passport on her, he could have taken her straight to the bloody airport without any of this ridiculous carrying on.

Think of the reward at the end, he reminded himself. In one week this would be over. It would all be over.

In seven days, his redemption would be complete.

CHAPTER THREE

EMILY SIGNED HER part of the agreement before they boarded the plane, refusing to climb the metal steps until Pascha had signed his part too. He'd typed it on his laptop on the drive to the airport, printing it off in the executive lounge. She'd also insisted on getting it witnessed by one of the flight crew.

One week of her life and her father's good name would be restored. He'd receive a quarter of a million pounds too, enough to see him through to old age. If he made it to old age, that was. At that moment, she wasn't prepared to take anything for granted when it came to her father. He was too fragile to look beyond the next day. Surely the anti-depressants would kick in soon?

She pushed aside thoughts that when her week was up she would likely find herself without a job. The odds were not in her favour. Hugo was temperamental at the best of times. All the leave

she'd had to take at the last minute recently, cou-
pled with her request not to travel outside the UK
for the foreseeable future, were strikes against
her name. A further week's leave without warning would be the final straw.

The moment they were airborne, she ignored
Pascha and tried to immerse herself in the fashion magazines she'd brought with her. Normally
she loved flipping through them, finding inspi-
ration in the most obscure things, but today she
couldn't concentrate. Her brain was too wired,
as if she'd had a dozen espressos in a row.

She'd known getting caught in Pascha's office
would have basic risks attached to it but she'd
assumed the worst that could happen would be a
night in a prison cell. She'd arranged for James to
spend the night with her father in that eventual-
ity. That particular risk had been worth it for the
chance of clearing her father's name and giving
him something that might, just might, give him
some form of hope to cling to. Something that
might prevent him from sinking another bottle
of Scotch and throwing dozens of pills down his
throat again.

Her father was broken. He'd given up.

She hadn't been a strong enough reason for him to want to live.

By the time they embarked onto the small luxury yacht in Puerto Rico that would take them on the last leg of their trip, Emily's brain hurt. Her heart hurt.

Leaving Pascha to talk safety issues with the yacht's skipper, in much the same way he'd discussed safety issues with the flight crew before they'd taken off from London, Emily settled onto a sofa in the saloon and closed her eyes, blinds shading her from the late-afternoon sun.

She must have fallen asleep as a tap on her shoulder made her open her eyes with a snap.

Pascha loomed over her. He wore the same outfit he'd been in when he'd caught her in his office hours earlier, but still looked as fresh as if he'd just dressed.

'We'll be there soon,' he said before turning round and heading back outside, leaving his dreadful citrus scent behind him. Okay, maybe it wasn't dreadful. Maybe it was actually rather nice. Too nice. It made her feel…hungry. She didn't want to like anything about him, not even his scent.

Despite her worry and lethargy, she couldn't help but experience a whisper of excitement when she joined him on deck and felt the warmth of the sun beat down on her face. It really was a picture-perfect scene. Not a single cloud marred the cobalt sky.

Pascha pointed out the tiny, verdant island before them poking out of the Atlantic—or was it the Caribbean? They were right at the border between the two watery giants. In the far distance she could see a cluster of larger islands, seemingly surrounding the smaller one like sentries.

'That is Aliana Island.' It was the first time he'd put a name to her final destination.

Aliana Island: even its name was beautiful.

Emily reminded herself that it should make no difference whether her prison for the next week was an under-stairs cupboard or a virtual paradise. Her reasons for being there were the same. She was there against her will.

All the same, the closer they got to their destination, the more her spirits lifted. The island didn't appear to get any bigger, but she could see more detail. The deep blue sea beneath them lightened, turning a clearer turquoise than she could have dreamed of, the sandy beach before them sparkling under the beaming sun.

'We have to be careful getting to the island,' Pascha explained in that clipped manner she was becoming used to. 'It's surrounded by a coral reef.'

'Aren't they dangerous for boats?' She didn't know much about coral reefs but that was one thing she was fairly certain of.

'Exceedingly dangerous,' he agreed. 'Only a fool would navigate coral waters without any prior knowledge of them. Luis has been navigating these waters for years.'

'That's good to know,' she murmured without surprise. In the short time she'd known him, Pascha had proved himself a man who took security and safety extremely seriously.

'Is that a temple?' she asked, spotting what looked like some kind of Buddhist retreat set back a little from the beach.

'No. It's my lodge.'

'*Your* lodge?'

'Aliana Island belongs to me.'

Despite herself, Emily was impressed. Looking carefully, she could see other, smaller buildings with thatched roofs branching off the main one. 'It's beautiful. How did it get its name? Was Aliana the person who discovered it?'

'No. Aliana is my mother.'

'Really?' Something flittered over her face, a look he couldn't discern but made him think his answer had pleased her somehow. 'You named an island after your mother? What a fabulous thing to do. I bet she was delighted when you told her, wasn't she?'

'She…'

He struggled to think of the correct wording to describe his mother's reaction—the slap across his face and the words, 'You think an *island* can repair the damage you caused?'

He decided on, 'She wasn't displeased.'

He'd bought the island three years before. The ink on the purchase contract had barely dried before he'd changed its name.

He'd had it all planned out. He would visit his mother and Andrei after five years of estrangement. As part of his atonement, he would invite them to spend a holiday with him on the island.

He would give them their own keys and tell them to think of it as theirs too—a special place for them all to share and use however they saw fit.

Time and distance had given him a great deal of perspective. When he closed his eyes, all he saw was the worry etched on his mother's face as she'd watched over the small son she hadn't known whether would live or die. He'd seen the stress Andrei had carried with him but had never shown his adopted son. The thick, dark hair had thinned and whitened too quickly; the capable hands had calloused seemingly overnight.

Fate had worked against him. Shortly before the lodge had been completed, before Pascha had been able to make things right between them, Andrei had died. He'd gone to bed and never woken up. A heart attack.

The man who'd raised him as if he were his own, who'd worked his fingers to the bone to give Pascha the chance to live, the man Pascha had walked away from…had gone. He'd lost the opportunity to apologise and make amends. He'd lost the opportunity to tell him that he loved him.

His grief-stricken mother…

Pascha's apology and remorse had washed right

over her. His words had come too late. He should have said them when Andrei was alive. Aliana Island was just a possession; it meant nothing to his mother, not when she no longer had her beloved husband to enjoy it with.

But, while he might never be able to make amends with Andrei personally, he could secure his legacy. It was the *only* thing he could do. And if he was successful...maybe then his mother would forgive him. Their relationship could be repaired—he had to believe that.

'Do you spend much time here?' Emily asked, thankfully moving the conversation onto safer territory.

'Not as much as I would like.'

The yacht had been brought into a lagoon and moored alongside a small jetty. A panelling in the side of the yacht unfurled to reveal metal steps for them to disembark from. Pascha strolled down the steps and made his way up the jetty.

He was sorely tempted to get Luis, the man he employed to skipper his yacht, to take him straight back to Puerto Rico so he could take his jet directly to Paris, his next destination. However, he'd been awake for over a day, having flown from Milan to London in the early hours. He needed sleep. If there was one thing Pascha did not mess around with, it was his health, and sleep was instrumental to it.

The odds of the illness which had threatened his life as a child returning was miniscule, but a miniscule chance was worse than no chance at all. Sleep, exercise and a healthy diet were all things he could control. Controlling them lowered that miniscule chance, putting the odds even more in his favour.

He'd planned to sleep on the flight from London but for once had been unable to, his awareness of the proximity of his guest having made it impossible for him to relax. He kept catching wafts of the perfume Emily had applied before he'd finally got her out of her bedroom. Her scent was delicious, an earthy smell with a touch of honeyed sweetness his senses responded to of their own accord, much to his annoyance.

He needed rest, and for that he'd need space. He would have a quick meal then get his head down— eight solid hours to recharge his batteries—then leave at first light.

He followed the pathway, traversing the beach

up to the main entrance of the lodge, aware of Emily following behind him. Valeria, his head of housekeeping, was there to greet them.

After exchanging pleasantries, he said, 'Please show Miss Richardson to her guest hut and show her whcrc everything is. Are we okay to eat in an hour?'

Valeria nodded. His unplanned visit hadn't fazed her in the slightest. Under normal circumstances Pascha would give proper notice of a planned visit so she could prepare for it. Today she'd had roughly twelve hours to get everything ready, but from what he could see everything was in hand.

When he stepped into his hut, everything was exactly as it should be, not a speck of dust to be seen. Before heading to the bathroom, he stepped out onto the veranda and breathed in the salty air, closing his eyes as he willed the usual peace he found on Aliana Island to envelope him.

With Emily Richardson there, he suspected peace would be a long way off.

If Emily's eyes were capable of widening any further, they would have. Connected to the main house by a set of dark hardwood stairs, her hut looked more like an enormous high-end luxury cabin than anything else, with floor-to-ceiling windows that opened up to give a panoramic view, not just of the island but the surrounding ocean. The entire front section of the hut was one huge sliding door. Steps led out to a private veranda with a dining table, then down to a balcony with an abundance of soft white sun-loungers. More steps led down onto the beach.

After a quick discussion about Emily's dietary requirements—apparently there were three chefs on site to prepare whatever she wanted, whenever she wanted—Valeria left her to settle in.

Alone, Emily tried to take it all in, but she was so overwhelmed by her hut, her surroundings, the fact that Aliana Island was a private paradise...

And this was her prison. A jail with a four-poster bed.

It felt as if she'd been plunged into the middle of a fantastical dream.

In the far corner of her hut was a roll-topped bath. She longed to get into it but felt too exposed with all the surrounding glass. Instead, she opted for a shower in her bathroom, which was mercifully private, then changed into a pair of three-quarter-length skinny black trousers with silver sequins running down the lines and a silky grey vest top. She applied her make-up with care. She'd always adored wearing make-up, loved the way it could enhance a mood. Today it felt as if she were applying battle armour.

Her appearance taken care of, she set about unpacking then padded out barefoot onto the veranda. Her spirits soared further when she found her own small private swimming pool. She'd caught a glimpse of the long pool that snaked around the main house, but to find she had her own one too...and one that was entirely private.

Now that she really took stock of everything, she could see she really did have complete privacy. No one could see into her space. She decided that she would definitely use the bath in the morning.

She checked herself, forcing a curb on her excitement. This was not a holiday. Not by a long mark. She must not forget that.

It wasn't until she leaned over the pebbled wall separating her balcony from the steps down to the beach that she caught a glimpse of another hut overhanging to the left of hers. Craning her neck for a better look, she jerked when she saw Pascha leaning over his own wall talking into his mobile phone, the top part of his naked torso visible…

He must have sensed her gaze for he suddenly looked down. For the briefest of moments their eyes locked before she tore her eyes away and stepped back, out of sight.

She inhaled deeply and placed a hand to her chest. Her heart raced, her skin tingled and, much as she tried to blink the image away, all she could see was the hard chest with a smattering of dark hair over taut muscles.

Utterly unnerved by her reaction to semi-naked Pascha, Emily resolved to stay in her hut for the rest of the evening, using its phone to call down to the kitchen and request her dinner be brought up to her.

It felt safer to keep out of his way. Much safer.

In the meantime, she needed to call home. But picking up the receiver proved a fruitless task. The phone in her hut connected to the main house but nowhere else. As soon as she dialled any other number, a beep rang in her ear. She was disappointed, but she wasn't surprised. The whole point in Pascha keeping her there was to stop her communicating with anyone. All the same, she decided to try her mobile phone. She curled up on an outdoor sofa that was completely hidden from view and switched it on. Nothing. No signal bars, no Internet access. Nothing. No wonder Pascha hadn't bothered trying to take it from her.

She muttered a curse just as a soft buzzer went off in her room.

'Come in,' she called, assuming it was her dinner being brought to her. Rising to her feet, she gave a sharp intake of breath when she found Pascha in her hut.

'How have you settled in?' he asked, stepping out to join her on the veranda. He'd changed into dark linen trousers and an open-necked light blue shirt. Were it not for the fact his attire had been ironed to within an inch of its life, and his hair styled to such an extent that not a single strand dared depart from the slight quiff, she would have said he looked casual. But then, casual was a state of mind. Emily doubted he ever switched off.

'I've settled in fine,' she replied, resisting the urge to push him back into the hut and shove him out through the French doors. It wouldn't make any difference if she did; they'd only be separated by the windows. She held her phone out to him. 'I need to call home.'

He didn't even look at it. 'There's a block on all electronic communications without an access code.'

'I gathered that. I need to call home. Is there another phone I can use?'

'You only left this morning.'

'A lot can happen in a day.' At his narrowing eyes, she quickly added, 'You can hover by my side while I make the call and satisfy yourself that I'm not revealing any state secrets. I just want to make sure my dad's okay and that my brother's got there.'

Silence hung between them while Pascha contemplated her request. After what felt like an age, he inclined his head. 'You can use my phone.'

'Seeing as *my* phone is useless here, I'll need a number my dad and brother can reach me on too.' She'd assumed he would take her phone and keep it on him, had assumed her family would be able to reach her even if she couldn't contact them.

When it looked as if he would refuse, she folded her arms. 'Look, you either let me give them an emergency contact number or I will make it my business to be the most difficult guest you've ever had here.'

'You're already the most difficult guest I've ever had here.' Was it her imagination or was that a glimmer of humour in his eyes?

'You haven't seen anything yet.'

'I can well believe it. You can call home and give my number as an emergency contact, but it can wait until after we've eaten.'

This time it was her eyes that narrowed.

His cheeks formed a semblance of a smile. 'Yes, Emily, you will be dining with me tonight.'

'I was planning on eating on my veranda. Alone,' she added pointedly.

'You can dine alone on your veranda for the rest of the week but this evening I require the pleasure of your company. My staff have set up the beach table for us.' From the way he enunciated the word 'pleasure', it was obvious he found the prospect of her company nothing of the sort.

'Why not?' She threw him a brittle smile. 'You and I are clearly ideal candidates for a romantic meal for two.'

His lips tightened. 'Circumstances are what they are. I'll be leaving for Paris first thing in the morning and there are a number of things we need to discuss before I leave.'

'Excellent.' She grinned at him without an ounce of warmth. 'Let's get this over with, then—with any luck it'll be the last time we have to suffer one another's company.'

CHAPTER FOUR

THE LONG TABLE on the beach had been set up for them just metres from the lapping waves of the ocean, tea-lights in lanterns glowing under the dusky sky.

'We're sitting on mats?' she asked, nodding at the thick cushions on the sand.

'Do you have a problem with that?'

She shrugged. 'No. I'm just surprised—I imagined you'd be averse to getting sand on your expensive clothes.'

'I find the sound of the ocean soothing,' he answered shortly. Emily's antagonism towards him was becoming trying. She had no one to blame for her predicament but herself. 'After the day I've had, I could use some respite.'

She settled onto a mat, tucking her bare feet beneath her. They really were the most delicate feet, he noticed: petite, much like the rest of her. Except her luscious mouth, of course.

He'd followed behind as they'd descended the stairs, holding onto the rail while she bounded down the steps without support, her long black hair, free from confinement, springing in all directions.

Emily had an energy about her that zinged. He found it intriguing. He found *her* intriguing. Any other woman in her predicament likely would have resorted to tears to get her own way. Emily had only become more defiant.

For the first time in a long time the image of Yana came into his mind, startling him. He never thought of his ex, had ruthlessly dispelled all memories of her so she was just a hazy figure in his past.

Yana and Emily were polar opposites, in looks and temperament.

The more time he spent with Emily, the more he was reminded of an uncut fire opal, passionate and vibrant. Yana was as polished as a Plushenko diamond. But by the time he'd ended their relationship she'd been a diamond without the lustre. And it had all been his fault.

He'd never had a problem attracting women but since he'd broken away from Andrei and set up on his own, building a multi-billion-dollar business in less than a decade, the feminine attention had become altogether hungrier. They were all wasting their time, something he spelt out at the outset of any fling. Sex was the most he could offer, the most he could give.

He'd destroyed the cut and polish of one woman. He would never put another in that position.

His thoughts were interrupted by a member of staff bringing out their starter of grilled squid and topping their wineglasses with chilled white before disappearing.

Pascha watched Emily take a bite, her lips moving in a way he could only describe as sensual. She really did have the sexiest of lips.

'What?' she asked a few moments later, looking at him quizzically.

To his chagrin, he realised he'd been too busy staring to take a bite of his own food.

He speared his fork into the delicate flesh of the squid. 'While you're staying here, I don't want you feeling you have to hide yourself away.'

'That won't be a problem when you've left. I'm looking forward to exploring your island.'

'Good.' It shouldn't bother him that she didn't want to be in his company. It *didn't* bother him. 'You'll find the island a place of hidden treasures. My staff are highly trained and able to cater for any wish you might have, which leads me to the next item on the agenda.'

'Do you want me to take minutes?'

'Excuse me?'

'You mentioned items on an agenda.' She put her knife and fork together and pushed her plate forward. 'Would you like me to act as secretary and write a set of minutes so neither of us forget what's discussed?'

Were it not for the unexpected spark of light that flashed in her eyes, he could have believed she was serious. 'I'm sure you'll remember it all without any problem.'

'A near compliment? I'm touched.'

His smile loosened a fraction. 'Onto my next item—my staff. I hand-picked them all and I do not want them upset in any shape or form.'

The spark of light in Emily's eyes vanished. 'My problem is with you, not your staff.'

'So long as you remember that. They follow my directives and know not to help you communicate with the outside world. Don't embarrass yourself or them by asking for their help.'

'I can go along with that so long as you promise to pass on any message from my family straight away.'

'If they get in touch once I've left the island, I will let Valeria know and she will pass on any message.'

'You'd better,' she muttered, becoming mute as staff inconspicuously cleared their starters away before returning with their main course. Soon, an array of fresh lobster, salads and spicy rice dishes was placed before them.

Emily heaped her plate with a little of everything then, using a bare hand, gripped the body of the lobster. Her eyes met his, insolence ringing from them as she reached for a claw with her other hand and twisted it off with a snap.

Pascha winced. While Emily attacked her lobster with relish, only using her crackers when absolutely necessary, Pascha used a more methodical approach, taking great care with the hard shell. By the time they'd finished eating, he was as clean as when he'd started, while her lips and fingers were slippery with butter.

His blood thickened as an image came into his mind of those slick fingers touching him…

What was it with this woman? Since he'd given Yana her freedom, he'd had more than his share of brief encounters, all with highly groomed, beautiful women who looked good on his arm. Not one of those women had roused him in anything other than the most basic of fashions. They certainly hadn't roused his senses. Not in the way Emily was doing at that moment and she wasn't even trying.

'Anything else you want to discuss?' she asked, pulling him out of his wayward thoughts. Bowls of hot flannels were placed before them and she took one, dabbing at her mouth, that beautiful, sensual mouth, and wiping her hands.

'No. That's everything.' There had been other issues but at that moment his brain felt as if a hazy fog had been tipped into it.

It was time to step away from this situation.

He should have got his staff to set up the dining hall, which had a table large enough to seat thirty. He should have stuck her right at the other end from him, all communication via megaphone.

If he hadn't wanted to eat by the ocean, he would have done just that, but in the morning he would leave for Paris, unlikely to return for a few months. There was something soothing about the sound of the gentle, rippling waves. It brought a contentment hc'd never found anywhere else, a knowledge that whatever he did and wherever his future lay the tides would still turn.

'In that case, let's move on to "any other business": my phone call home.' She held a hand out, palm up. 'You gave me your word.'

He had to admire her devotion to her father. Such intense loyalty, she'd been prepared to spend a night in a police cell for it. It almost made him forgive that it had been *his* office she'd broken into and *his* data she'd attempted to steal. Almost.

Where had his own loyalty been eight years ago? He'd put his pride first and now it was too late. Andrei had died estranged from the adopted son he'd once adored. Was it any wonder his mother couldn't forgive him?

Snapping himself out of the settling melancholy, he pulled his smart phone out of his pocket and keyed in the password. 'What's the number?'

She recited it from memory. As soon as he heard the tone connecting the two lines, he passed it to her. She practically snatched it from him and pressed it to her ear.

'James?' Emily couldn't hide her relief. Her brother was there.

After hearing that her father had refused to get out of bed for his dinner, never mind eat it, Emily's eyes darted back to Pascha, who was watching her.

There were so many more questions she wanted to ask, but she resisted.

Now was not the time, not with Pascha listening in so closely. It was one thing for people to know how ill her father was, but his suicide attempt... No; that was between James, her and the medical profession. When her father recovered—and he would; whatever it took to get him better she would do it—she didn't want him living with the stigma of being the man who'd tried to kill himself. He wouldn't want it for himself. When he was well, his pride was everything. It had always been that way.

'My phone hasn't got a signal here,' she lied to her brother. 'So use this number if there's an emergency. It's right there in front of you on caller display—write it down, James. By the way, has Hugo called?' She didn't know if it was relief or dread she felt when James replied in the negative.

Disconnecting the call, she handed the phone back.

Her chest felt full and heavy and she suddenly realised she was on the verge of tears.

'Who is Hugo?' Pascha asked. 'You mentioned him earlier.'

Emily sighed.

'Hugo is my boss. Or perhaps I should say *was* my boss.'

Pascha arched a brow. *'Was?'*

'Unless Hugo's had a new heart transplanted into him, I won't have a job to go back to. Most employers wouldn't be happy about a key member of staff taking off for a week's leave on a whim, especially when that member of staff has already been given an official warning for taking too many unauthorised absences.' Stopping herself, Emily clamped her lips together. Pascha didn't care about her or her job. All she was to him was a potential threat that had to be hidden away.

Fashion design was all she'd ever wanted to do. But she shouldn't complain about Hugo. He'd been incredibly supportive through what had been a horrific time, at least initially, but he had a business to run—something he'd made abundantly clear when he'd given her that official warning less than a month ago.

After a long, thoughtful pause, Pascha said in a softer tone, 'I'm certain that if you explain the situation when you return Hugo will understand. He must know how ill your father is.'

Emily felt her heart lurch at the unexpected kindness from Pascha. Heartlessness she could cope with, but not that. Not now when her stomach felt so knotted she was having trouble holding down the beautiful food she'd just eaten.

Her mother had adored lobster, had been the person to teach her how to demolish one so effectively.

A wave of despair almost had her doubled over, lancing her stomach with a thousand thorns.

Her darling, darling mother; oh, how she *missed* her.

Emily fought to control her emotions. She couldn't let him see it. She just couldn't. He had enough power over her already.

'I…I need to get some sleep,' she said, backing away from him. 'Was there anything else you wanted?'

He shook his head, a strange, penetrative expression in his eyes.

She gave a brief nod and turned on her heel, forcing her rubbery legs to walk.

By the time Emily slid the door of her cabin shut, the grief had abated and her sudden tears had retreated back into their ducts.

Sinking onto the bed, she gazed up at the ceiling.

She could still feel Pascha's gaze on her skin.

The next morning, fortified by a huge breakfast that had been brought to her room, and armed with mosquito repellent, high-factor sun-cream and bottles of water, Emily set off to explore the island. It had been a long evening and an even longer night. She'd gone to bed far earlier than she usually did. As hard as she'd tried she'd been unable to sleep, her mind a cacophony of faces clamouring for attention: her mother; her father; her brother. Pascha…

She'd felt trapped in her guest lodge. She might be free to go anywhere on the island but knowing she could bump into Pascha had kept her firmly inside. She couldn't even get her sewing machine out. Such was the absolute silence of the island, the noise would have woken everyone up.

Making her way out of the main living area, she passed dozens of workers bustling around cleaning the house and grounds, the place a hive of activity. First she traversed the beach, smiling to see a couple of small children chasing each other over the sand. She waved politely at Luis, who was at the bow of the yacht at the jetty. He must have returned from taking Pascha to Puerto Rico.

Now she knew Pascha was off the island she could breathe a little easier, and was already plotting ways to convince Valeria to let her phone England and check on her father. So what if she embarrassed herself? Some things were more important than saving face.

She'd even tried to crack the code used to block her mobile again. It had been a complete waste of time. She doubted even her old housemate, the whizz who had taught her how to hack into Pascha's laptop, could have cracked it.

Finished with the beach, she set off up through the dense foliage. The further inland she went, the greater the humidity, and the trail she followed seemed to go nowhere in particular.

On the verge of turning back, she heard the sound of rushing water.

A couple of minutes later, she was awestruck with wonder.

'Oh wow,' she whispered under her breath.

She had reached a vast, open area with the middle missing, as if a huge circular section had been dug out of it. On the other side of the bottomless circle ran gushing water, pouring over the edge like a sheet. A ledge jutted out on her side. She stepped onto it and peered over. She'd found the bottom. The drop was at least forty feet, the waterfall pouring into a large, round pool.

Almost hugging herself with joy, she sat with her legs dangling over the ledge and took a long drink of water. She wished she'd taken Valeria up on her offer of a packed lunch. She could happily spend the next week in this little spot of paradise.

She'd found a spot very similar to this a few years before, on a holiday in Thailand. She and the friends she'd travelled with had taken it in turns to jump into the pool, exulting at the weightlessness of the fall. Emily hadn't had a care in the world. Not then.

Whipping her flip-flops and T-shirt off, leaving just her bikini top and shorts, she slathered herself in sun-cream and rested back, happy simply to soak it all in. Her solitude didn't last nearly long enough.

The shuffling of movement made her start. Turning her head, all her contentment died to see Pascha standing behind her.

'What are you doing here?' she asked rudely. He should be snug in his jet, flying away across the ocean.

Dressed in a pair of knee-length, dark-beige canvas shorts and an unbuttoned black polo shirt, he really was incredibly handsome. Even with his hair perfectly in place, and his clothes pressed to within an inch of their lives, he looked far more human than in his business attire. Her eyes drifted down to his calves, something hot flushing through her at their muscularity and the fine, dark hairs covering them. 'I thought you'd gone to Paris.'

'Never mind that, come away from the edge.' Speaking of edges, there was a definite one in his voice.

'I'm perfectly happy where I am, thank you.' Well, she had been.

'Where you're sitting could break away. It isn't safe.'

'Worried I might fall? At least it will save you having to worry about keeping me here.'

'Don't be infantile.' His face contorted into something resembling anger. 'While you're on this island your safety is my responsibility.'

'Actually,' she said, adopting an airy tone, 'I think you'll find I'm a fully grown woman and perfectly capable of taking responsibility for my own safety.'

'Not on my watch.'

'Have you jumped into the pool yet?' she asked, although she already suspected what the answer would be.

'That's a ridiculous question.'

'It feels like flying.' She couldn't help the wistfulness that came into her voice. 'It feels like nothing else on this earth.'

'I couldn't care what it feels like. It's dangerous. Now, come off that ledge—you won't be of any use to your father if you hurtle to your death.'

Damn him.

For a few brief moments she'd forgotten what her life had become, had slipped back into a life that had been free of worry and responsibility.

But he was right. What *would* become of her father if anything were to happen to her? What would become of James? James was more than capable of caring for their dad with her instruction, but when it came to working the practicalities out for himself he was useless.

Only a year ago she would have held her ground and refused anything other than taking a running jump off the ledge and plunging into the deep pool below.

As she now knew, through painful experience, a lot could happen in a year. A lot *had* happened. Her whole world had been ripped apart.

Pascha watched as a host of emotions flittered

over Emily's pretty face. It had been a low blow using her father to make her see sense, but until she came away from that ledge he knew his racing pulse wouldn't rest. Perspiration ran down his back that had nothing to do with the soaring temperature.

But, when she shuffled back and got to her feet, the heat he felt under the collar of his polo shirt surged. Suddenly, now she was safe, the bikini top and shorts Emily wore came firmly onto his radar.

Her ebony hair was piled on top of her head, ringlets spiralling, but she'd left her face free of make-up, her beauty shining through in a wholly disturbing way. And that body… Skin that looked like silk…

As quickly as the snap of his fingers, his pulse raced anew, his blood thickening.

There was nothing immodest about Emily's khaki bikini; compared to the scraps of candy-floss most women of his acquaintance liked to wear, it was demure. The black shorts she wore with them were figure-hugging but modest. She wasn't wearing anything he hadn't seen hundreds of women wear on beaches around the world, yet she was the only one he reacted to with such force.

Breathing slowly through his teeth, he willed away his completely inappropriate reaction to her. 'Get your shoes on—we're going back.'

Dark-brown eyes narrowing, she folded her arms across her delicious chest. 'I've moved away from the ledge but I'm not prepared to let you order me around any further. If you want to go back, then go ahead. I'm staying here.'

'You haven't eaten for hours. My chefs are preparing a late lunch for us. You can come back here later if you must.'

Something sharp pierced into Emily's chest.

'Give me a sec,' she said, looking away from him and slipping her toes into her silver sparkly flip-flops.

Had he *really* tracked her down just to make sure she had something to eat?

The last person to care that she ate three square meals a day had been her mother. During their daily phone calls she would always ask what Emily had eaten that day, what she was planning for her dinner…

Shaking her head to clear it of despondency,

she shrugged her rucksack over her shoulder and followed Pascha back through the trail.

'So why are you still here?' she asked after a few minutes of silence. Despite his much longer strides, he never went too far ahead. She took a swig of water. The heat within the dense canopy of trees was fast becoming insufferable.

He ducked under an overhanging branch. 'There's a problem with the engine of the yacht. We need to wait for a part to be delivered from the mainland.'

'How long will that take?'

'It should be here by the end of the day.'

'Excellent. So you'll be leaving for Paris before the evening?'

'Sorry to disappoint you, but the part needs to be installed and then checked for safety before I allow anyone to go anywhere in it. I should be able to get away in the morning, depending on what the weather's like. There's a tropical storm heading for the Caribbean. I won't leave until it's passed.'

Emily didn't like the sound of that. 'Are we in its path?'

'No. We're likely only to get some high winds

and rain at some point this evening, but it's an uncertain situation…'

Before he could finish his sentence, Emily lost her footing, practically skiing down a particularly steep incline.

Her cheeks were crimson; the only saving grace was that she hadn't fallen flat on her face.

'Are you okay?' Pascha asked, surefootedly hurrying to her side.

'Yes, yes. No harm done.' Feeling like the biggest fool in the world, she accepted his help, allowing his large, warm fingers to wrap around her own and pull her back to her feet.

'Thank you,' she muttered, knowing her cheeks had turned an even deeper shade of red that had nothing to do with embarrassment.

She snatched her hand away from his, as if the action could eradicate the effects of his touch. It felt as if he'd magically heated her skin, his clasp sending tiny darts of energy zinging through her veins, making her heart pump harder.

Pascha was still staring at her intently.

'Are you sure you're all right?' he asked after too long a pause.

'Honestly, I'm fine.' To prove it, she started

walking again. It was with relief that she spotted the roof of the main cabin of the lodge poking through the foliage.

'Are you sure you haven't hurt yourself?'

'I *said* I'm fine.'

Before he had a chance to quiz her further, the theme to a cartoon she'd adored in childhood rang out. To her utter amazement, she realised it was his phone ringing.

Pascha had the theme to *Top Cat* as his ringtone?

He pressed it to his ear. 'Da?' His eyes immediately switched to her face. 'Yes, she is right with me. One moment.' He handed the phone to her, mouthing, 'Your brother,' as he did so.

Her blood turned to ice.

'James?' The coldness quickly subsided when she learned the reason for her brother's call. He couldn't work the washing machine. Their mother had always done it for him, even after he'd left the family home. Since she'd died he'd used a laundry service—after failing to cajole Emily into doing it for him.

By the time she ended the call, irritation suffused her. She'd explicitly told him only to call in a genuine emergency—one call too many and for all she knew Pascha might decide not to bother passing on any messages. It was pure luck that she'd been with him at that moment.

Still, she consoled herself, at least she wouldn't have to badger Valeria for use of the lodge phone for another day. James had assured her their father's condition was the same, so that was one less thing to worry about.

Pascha had listened to Emily's side of the conversation with increasing incredulity. 'Your brother called about a *washing machine*?'

Judging by the way she inhaled deeply and swallowed, it was obvious Emily was carefully choosing her words. 'James isn't the most domestic of people.'

'Doing the laundry does not require a PhD.'

'In my brother's eyes, it does. Anyway, how would you know? I bet you've never used a washing machine in your life.'

'I make a point of learning how to use all the domestic appliances in my homes,' Pascha told her coldly. He understood why she made so many assumptions about him but it needled all the same. He hadn't been born rich—quite the opposite. Everything he had he'd worked damned hard for. Just being here, being alive, had been the hardest battle of all.

'Why would you do that?' For once there was no sarcasm or anything like it in her tone, just genuine curiosity. 'Surely you have a fleet of staff in all your homes?'

'I like to take care of myself,' he said tightly. 'Aliana Island is different—I come here to get away from the world and switch off.'

The lodge was only a few yards ahead of them now. Emily slowed down to adjust her rucksack. 'I can see why you would do that,' she admitted. 'I think Aliana Island might be the most beautiful spot on the planet.'

'I think that too.'

She gave him something that looked like the beginning of a genuine smile, her eyes crinkling a touch at the corners. It sent the most peculiar sensation fluttering in his chest. Before he had a chance to analyse it, he spotted Valeria waving at him in the distance.

'Excuse me,' he said, 'But work calls.'

As he walked, that same strange fluttering sensation stayed with him.

CHAPTER FIVE

EMILY HAD A quick shower, then steeled herself before setting off to the main lodge. But, when she stepped in the dining hall, the table was set for one.

A curious emptiness settled in her stomach when a young girl—she was certain the girl was Valeria and Luis's daughter—brought a bowl of bisque and some warm rolls through to her and gave a garbled apology about something important Pascha needed to attend to.

She ate mechanically then retired back to her hut, distantly aware the island's staff was now out in force. Though they weren't bustling in the sense that people bustled in large cities, the speed with which they were working had increased dramatically.

Back at her lodge, Emily dragged her sewing machine out and placed it on the table then got her tubes of fabric and her A5 pad of designs.

What she really needed but had forgotten to bring was a mannequin on which to pin the dress she wanted to make. She wondered if Valeria's daughter—she must learn her name—would model for her.

Finally she had enough time on her hands to turn her own designs into something. Her own creations. Her own visions. No Hugo demanding she focus solely on *his*.

Disregarding the lack of mannequin and model, Emily laid the fabric on the long table and began to make her marks. How long ago had she designed this dress? Over a year, at the very least, before the bottom of her world had dropped away from her and she'd been left floundering, clinging on to anything that would give her a purpose.

The past year had been a constant whirl of hospital trips and visits to the family home. She'd been desperate to care for and spend as much time with her mother before the inevitable happened. All of this on top of holding down a demanding job and looking after her own home. When the inevitable had happened, life had continued at the same pace, this time a whirl of funeral arrangements, form filling and taking care of her increasingly fragile father. There had been no time to switch off. There had been no time for herself.

She placed the fabric chalk under her nose and inhaled, squeezing her eyes tight as memories of sitting in her mother's craft study assailed her. Her mother would have loved the opportunity to be a seamstress but it had never been an option for her. She'd married at eighteen and had had her first child at nineteen, devoting herself to being a good wife and mother.

And she had been. Even if Emily had been given a city of women to choose a mother from, Catherine Richardson would be the one she'd have chosen. Always supportive, always loving. When Emily had won her place at fashion college, she doubted there had been a prouder mother alive.

She wished her mother was here with her to see this beautiful island. But of course, if that awful, awful disease hadn't claimed her mother, Emily would never have seen Aliana Island either.

Catherine Richardson's death had unhinged the entire family and, no matter what Emily did or how hard she tried, she couldn't fix it back together.

She couldn't fix this dress either. She'd finished her markings but without a model or a mannequin she would be sewing blind.

How could she not have thought to bring a mannequin with her when she'd remembered everything else?

Sighing, she gathered all her stuff back together and put it neatly away before wandering out onto the veranda.

As she leaned over the wall, she couldn't help but peek up to her left, where Pascha's hut jutted out. Nothing. If he was in there, he was out of sight.

She forced her attention onto the calm blue lagoon before her and breathed in the salty air which, mingled with the mass of sweet frangipani growing everywhere, created the most magical scent. If she could bottle it, she would make a fortune. She wanted to be out there in it.

She'd been shown a huge wooden hut that held a host of items for outdoor entertainment. She'd been told she could use whatever she liked when the mood took her. It was kept unlocked. She skipped down from her cabin and let herself in. Tennis and badminton rackets, sets of boules and kites all lay neatly shelved amongst kayaks and surfboards. So orderly was it all that she found what she was looking for with no effort at all: a row of snorkels and flippers.

Kitted out, she headed for the lagoon, delighting to feel the warmth of the fine white sand between her toes and the beam of the sun heating her skin, a breeze tempering it enough to make it bearable. In the distance, a boat sailed away from the island, going quickly enough soon to be a speck on the horizon.

Just one day in paradise and she had to admit she was already revising her opinion of the sun. Beneath the top heated layer, the water in the lagoon was deliciously cool, and she waded out in her flippers to waist height before donning the snorkel and diving under the surface.

What a sight there was to behold. She'd seen so many pictures in the media of coral reefs dying, but here it thrived—blooms of colour in all shapes and sizes, an abundance of fish and other marine creatures, their individual colours and features clearly delineated.

Utter heaven.

Sitting on the ledge earlier overlooking the waterfall, she'd felt a sense of peace. She felt that same tranquillity now. It was just her and the lagoon. Nothing else. Down here, the rest of the world might not exist, and she was going to revel in the feeling. Even if just for a short while.

Emily's hut was still empty.

Pascha swore under his breath.

He'd searched the rest of the lodge. He needed to speak to her and she'd done another disappearing act. The only place now he could think she might be was at the waterfall she'd been so enamoured with. It was a good forty-minute walk, which wasn't the greatest length of time, but with the latest weather developments every second was precious.

Stepping out onto her veranda, he spotted the figure far out in the lagoon. He didn't even have to blink to know it was her.

Pascha cursed again, descending the outdoor stairs that led to the beach at a much quicker rate than usual.

In an ideal world he would send someone else

out to her, but to do so would be to tear a member of his staff away from jobs that were now being undertaken as a matter of urgency.

As soon as he reached the sand, he kicked his deck shoes off.

After far too long standing, waiting vainly for her to notice him, he sat down and stripped off his polo shirt, ready to swim out to her. Except during that small action she'd disappeared from view.

Where was she?

Eyes narrowed in concentration, he scoured the area she'd been but could see no sign of her. His heart thudded harder. Where was she?

And then she emerged feet from the shoreline.

For the briefest of moments, his heart stopped.

Emily was wearing the same modest khaki bikini she'd worn earlier but she'd removed the shorts to reveal brief bikini bottoms. She'd donned a white T-shirt—sensible in this heat; he would give her credit for that—but the water made it transparent, the material clinging to her like a second skin.

He didn't think he'd ever witnessed such an erotic sight. Her dripping hair was longer than he could have imagined, the water pulling her curls out so it hung in a long sheet down to the small of her back.

Unable to tear his eyes away from the tantalising sight before him, his mouth went dry and heat pooled in his groin.

It wasn't until she started wringing water from her hair that she noticed him.

Something that was a cross between a scowl and a smile played on her lips as she removed the flippers and headed over to him.

'Come out to play?'

Mouth dry, he swallowed and shook his head, partly to refute her question and partly to clear it from the haze that had engulfed it.

He wanted to reach out a hand to her waist and pull her down to him. He wanted to roll her onto the sand and…

'Next time you decide to go out into the lagoon, make sure you let someone know,' he said in a far harsher tone than he'd intended.

Suddenly he felt furious. He should be in Paris finalising the documents that would make the completion of the Plushenko deal a formality, not worrying about the safety of the woman whose actions had been the catalyst preventing him from being *in* Paris. He certainly shouldn't be fantasising about making love to her, and *certainly* not right now when there was an emergency afoot.

She eyed him coolly before a tight, emotionless smile formed on her face and, so quickly that he had no time to react, she gathered her thick hair together and wrung it out again, this time over him, cold droplets falling onto his chest.

He jumped back. 'What did you do that for?'

'Because I felt like it,' she answered with a shrug. 'And because I've possibly just spent the most relaxing, wonderful hour of my entire life and you've ruined my mood completely with your irrational sanctimony.'

'I am being neither irrational nor sanctimonious.' He gritted his teeth together. He would hold on to his temper if it killed him. 'Anything could have happened to you out there. You might have got cramp...'

'Anything *could* have happened, but it didn't.'

'But if it had there would have been no one there to help you. In future, I would appreciate it if you let someone know when you're planning an activity with danger attached to it.'

Her eyes held his, narrowing, studying him, before he caught an imperceptible shift in them, as if they'd melted a little. Her clamped lips relaxed, a wry smile playing on the corners. 'Message received.'

'Good.' All the same, he made a mental note to warn his staff to keep an extra eye on her. Emily had a reckless streak in her. He would not have anything happen to her when she was on his island and under his protection.

'Was there a particular reason you sought me out? Or are you just stalking me? Only, it's the second time you've come looking for me today.'

He ignored her flippancy. 'The tropical storm I mentioned earlier has changed paths—only slightly, but it's now heading for us.' He'd been given the news on his way to the dining hall.

She blanched and tilted her face upwards. 'I thought it felt a little breezy.'

The wind was slowly picking up speed, a few tendrils of her drying hair lifting with the breeze.

'These storms can turn from nothing to something very quickly.'

A sharp breath escaped her pretty lips. 'Okay, so what do we do?'

'What we do is go to safety,' he said grimly.

'Are we leaving the island?'

'No. We have the necessary shelter and provisions here.'

'The way you were talking, it was as if we had to move to safety now.'

'We do. The ocean currents are already strengthening. I've sent the last of my staff who live on the neighbouring islands home so they can be with their families, but the rest of us need to move to higher ground.'

Emily had been a touch sceptical about Pascha's insistence that they head straight for the shelter. Now she understood. The weather was changing far too quickly, even for her liking.

When they'd started walking the trail, a different path to the one she'd followed to the waterfall, the sun still blazed down on them. They finished guided by Pascha's powerful torch.

He'd insisted she carry a torch too, which she'd nestled in her rucksack with the few other items he'd permitted her to bring to the shelter. He'd chivvied her along in her hut, glaring at her while she'd debated what she needed to take.

In the end, he'd snapped with exasperation, 'The lodge and its huts are designed to the highest of standards. The chances of it sustaining any significant damage are very slim. Your possessions will be fine.'

'Then why are we going somewhere else for shelter?' she'd asked.

'Because a slim chance is worse than no chance. The shelter's on high ground and is designed to withstand the worst the weather can throw at us. I can guarantee your safety there.'

The wind had picked up as they walked but had no more strength than a mildly blustery English day. She knew this would increase, could feel it in the air around her. And she could see it. It wasn't yet full sunset but thick, black clouds covered what was left of the sun, the previously cobalt sky now a dismal dark grey.

Yet, now she saw the fortress he'd brought her to, she felt total confidence they would make it through the night unscathed, at least in terms of any damage by the storm. The shelter was a small concrete building in a small clearing, close enough to be protected by the surrounding trees but far enough not to sustain any real damage should any of them fall. When she followed Pascha inside, she was further encouraged that no damage could befall them, the interior walls of the shelter being reinforced steel.

But whether or not a night spent here presented dangers of a different sort…

'Where's everyone else?' The lodge had been deserted when they'd set off up the trail.

'They've gone to their own shelter.'

'What, this one is just for you and me?'

Pascha nodded, his mouth still set in the grim line it had held for the past couple of hours.

'Why didn't you tell me it would be just the two of us sharing?' she asked, not bothering to hide her irritation.

'I didn't think it important.'

'Well, *I* do. If you'd told me, I could have camped out with Valeria and the rest of the staff in their shelter.'

He raised a bored brow. 'My staff are all, in one way or another, extended family to each other. I deliberately built them their own shelter so in events like this they could be together *as* a family. You might be a guest, and I might be their boss, but they deserve their privacy away from us.'

How could she possibly argue with that? Although, she wanted to. She *really* wanted to. Sharing a confined space with Pascha for the foreseeable future could only bring trouble.

The interior of the shelter was practical but luxurious, with a large double bed, a plush sofa, a dining table and a small kitchenette with a bar at the end. The only privacy came in the form of a bathroom which was, by anyone's standards, opulent.

When Pascha shut the door of the shelter, the silence was total, making Emily realise just how loud the wind had become.

She peered through a small round window which reminded her of a ship's porthole, the only source of natural light in the shelter.

Shelter? It was the same size as her London flat.

Turning her head, she found him opening cupboards and rummaging through drawers.

'Can I get you a drink?' he asked, not looking at her.

Taken aback at the offer, she stared at him. 'What have you got?'

'Everything.'

'Rum and Coke?' she said flippantly, wanting to test him.

His grey eyes met hers. 'Do you want ice in that?'

'Seriously?'

He reached under the bar and pulled out a bottle of rum, arching a brow as he displayed it for her.

She had to admit, she was impressed. And an alcoholic drink might take the edge off her angst. *Might.* 'No ice for me, thank you.'

'A thank you? You shock me.'

'I like to keep you on your toes.'

'You're doing an excellent job of it.'

While Pascha mixed them both a drink, her curiosity overcame her and she wandered into the kitchenette to rifle through the cupboards.

Amazing. There was enough food here for them to live like kings for at least a fortnight. A month, if they downgraded to princes.

'I take it there's a back-up generator?' she said.

'Of course.'

Something in his tone made her look at him. He looked furious. 'What's the matter?'

'I've left my phone charger at the lodge.'

'And?'

'And I don't have enough battery left to get through the night.'

'I would suggest going back for it but looking at the trees through the window I can see it wouldn't be the brightest of moves.'

'Finally she says something sensible.'

'*I* didn't leave the charger behind so don't take it out on me.' She wasn't any happier about it than he was—what if there was an emergency at home? James wouldn't be able to get hold of her.

She forced herself to think practically. If an emergency did occur, she wouldn't be able to do anything about it anyway, not from Aliana Island.

A whole evening of peace.

She couldn't even bring herself to feel guilty about it. Peace had become such an elusive thing in her life.

It was just a shame she had to spend it with Pascha Virshilas. It would be more relaxing to spend it with an angry bear. Though she had to concede that an angry bear wouldn't have the sex appeal...

Where had *that* thought popped out from?

No, no, no. If she was going to get through the night with even a semblance of sanity left, she had to tune out the fact she was in a confined space with the sexiest man alive.

Sexiest man alive?

Ten minutes in the shelter and she was clearly suffering from cabin fever.

'I'm not taking it out on you,' Pascha said.

'Good,' she shot back, the scowl on her face still evident.

He expelled a long breath and ran his fingers through his hair. Technically speaking, it wasn't Emily's fault, but if he hadn't been so determined to get her to the safety of the shelter, and wasted all that time at the beach with her, he would never have forgotten something as vital as his phone charger.

He could kick himself. He *should* kick himself.

Pascha should be with his lawyers. They'd spoken and corresponded throughout the day, none of them prepared to leave anything to chance, but it wasn't the same as being in the same room.

There was too much that could go wrong and scupper the Plushenko deal, and he was thousands of miles away. And soon he'd be totally cut off from all communication.

He finished mixing her drink and handed it to her.

'Thank you.' She turned away and strolled into the living area. Her behind really did sway beautifully when she walked, he noticed, curving nicely in her modest shorts and causing a whole heap of improper thoughts to race through him. Those improper thoughts were not helped by her silver top with its slanting neckline, which displayed a whole heap of porcelain shoulder, transparent enough for him to see the bikini she wore beneath it.

'So, what is there to do for entertainment in here?' she asked briskly, curling up on the sofa.

He held back the answer that formed on his tongue by the skin of his teeth. 'I'm sure a resourceful woman like you can make her own entertainment.'

She took a sip of her drink. 'Maybe enough of these will send me to sleep and then I'll be able to wake up and the storm will be over.'

'You'll have a headache if you drink too many of them.'

'Then I'll take a headache tablet.'

The woman had an answer for everything.

'Are you hungry?'

Her face scrunched up. 'A bit.'

'I'm not the greatest of cooks but I know how to make eggs on toast. Do you want some?'

She jumped back to her feet. 'I tell you what, I'll cook.'

'Can you cook?' Why did that surprise him?

'Yep. It'll give me something to do.'

'Are you bored?'

'Yep. Anything you don't like to eat?'

'I'll eat anything.'

She practically skipped to the kitchenette. Opening the cupboards and the fridge, she started examining ingredients, selecting some, rejecting others.

'Don't get too excited,' she warned. 'I can cook but it won't be the *haute cuisine* you're used to.'

'I didn't grow up eating *haute cuisine*,' he said drily.

'Someone with three chefs at his holiday island is not someone who eats simple food.'

He'd followed her to the kitchenette and his huge form blocked her way to the utensil cupboard. A masculine scent with a hint of citrus filled her senses.

'Excuse me,' she muttered.

He shifted to the left.

Emily knelt down and snatched at a saucepan, tugged it out and immediately lost her grip, the pan clanging to the floor.

She picked it up and shoved it on the work surface. 'Look, you're getting under my feet. Why don't you sit down while I get on with dinner?'

What was *wrong* with her? Her entire body was flushed, as if she'd been heated from the inside out; her hands and fingers were refusing to cooperate with her brain.

The only thing she knew with any certainty was that this was going to be a long night.

CHAPTER SIX

EMILY DID HER best to eat her dinner but she struggled to swallow.

Her body just wouldn't relax.

What she needed was noise. She liked noise. It was comforting. If she'd been eating at her flat or at her parents' house—correction, her dad's house—the radio would be humming in the background.

Here, in the shelter, there was nothing but silence. Heavy, oppressive silence.

'Are you not enjoying your meal?' Pascha asked her.

Looking down, she found she'd been pushing her pasta around her plate.

'I'm not very hungry,' she confessed, adding with forced brightness, 'They always say the chef loses their appetite when it comes to the actual eating.'

'Well, I think it's delicious,' he said, popping a

heaped forkful of her pasta concoction into his mouth to make his point.

She couldn't help but smile, but as the corners of her mouth lifted nodules in her belly tightened.

How could she eat when Pascha sat so close, near enough that if she moved her foot forward an inch she would graze his leg?

She was softening towards him. She could feel it. And she didn't like it one jot. It felt disloyal, as if she was somehow betraying her father by finding the enemy to be so human. *And so damn sexy…*

However it was dressed up, be it mutual blackmail or force, Pascha had given her no choice but to come to Aliana Island. There had been no option but for her to comply. Her desperate attempt to help her father had backfired so spectacularly, a firework could be made in its honour.

And yet in the short time they'd been together Pascha had shown more consideration towards her than she'd ever known. He'd sought her out at the waterfall because he'd been worried she would be hungry. He'd sought her out at the lagoon because of the storm, because he'd wanted to take her to safety. Even his anger at her snorkelling alone had been provoked by his concern for her well-being.

When had anyone last worried about her safety? *When had anyone last worried about her full-stop?*

For her own sanity she needed to hold onto her anger towards him.

But how could she hold onto her anger and hate when every time she looked up at him she found magnetic grey eyes holding hers and the nodules in her belly tightened that little bit more?

She waited until he'd cleared his plate before rising.

'Sit down and relax,' he said, gathering the plates together. 'You've done your share. I'll clear up.'

Only when his back was turned to her at the kitchenette did she exhale. It felt as if she'd been holding her breath the entire meal.

As she watched him load the dishwasher, admiring the tautness of his buttocks against the heavy cotton of his shorts, the strangest feeling crept through her veins, a fizzing, as if her blood had awoken and started dancing.

Disturbed by all these strange feelings being evoked within her, and determined to pull herself together, Emily decided she might as well take Pascha's advice and relax. Taking another sip of wine, she put her bare feet up on his recently vacated chair.

'You would make an excellent house-husband,' she commented idly. He was wiping the work surface down with such thoroughness, she wouldn't be surprised if the top layer was scrubbed away.

He gave a grunt.

'I take it the thought of being a house-husband does nothing for you?' Saying the words made her realise she knew nothing about his private life. Nothing. Was there a woman? Surely there must be? Regardless of his wealth, a man who looked like Pascha would attract pretty much any woman he fixed those grey eyes on.

Another grunt.

'Do you think you'll ever marry?' she asked.

Pascha paused from wiping the side down to pin her with a stare. 'What's with all the questions?'

'I'm bored,' she lied with a shrug. 'You're the

one who dragged me to a shelter where there's nothing to do to pass the time.'

'Can't you be bored quietly?'

'Why? Am I annoying you?'

'Yes.'

'Good.'

His glare turned into a half-smile and a rueful shake of the head.

'So are you going to answer my question?'

'The answer is no. No, I don't think I'll ever marry. In fact, I know I won't.'

'That sounds pretty emphatic.'

'That's because it is.'

'Why don't you want to get married?'

He turned his head to spear her with a glance. 'Why don't you have a man in *your* life?' he countered. 'How long have *you* been single?'

'Seven years.'

He leaned back against the work surface and folded his arms. 'That long?'

'Yep.'

'Any flings?'

'Nope. I work in the fashion industry. The vast majority of the single men I work with are gay. It's rare I meet an eligible straight man.' She tried her best to keep her tone light and nonchalant. Okay, so she was exaggerating, but it was the old tried and tested response she'd been using for years. Anything had to be better than admitting she'd given up finding anyone who didn't make her feel inadequate. Who didn't make her feel second-best.

She'd long accepted love would never happen for her. She'd grown tired of trying to find it. When her father had sunk into the dark depressions that had blighted her childhood, it had always been her mother who'd lifted him out of it, never his daughter. When he was at his lowest ebb, Emily might not exist. She'd never doubted his love for her but it had never been enough. *She* wasn't enough. His suicide attempt had only reinforced that feeling. If she wasn't enough to make her own father want to live, how could she possibly be enough for someone else?

And, just like that, the lighter mood she'd been trying to create darkened, making her stomach cramp.

Time to move onto safer territory, far away from relationships of any form.

'Seeing as the subjects of marriage and relationships bring us both out in a cold sweat, why don't you tell me why you want to buy Plushenko's instead? My guess is that it has to be personal.'

'What makes you think that?'

'You don't force a woman to travel halfway round the world simply to salvage a deal without it being personal.'

Although the very mention of the word Plushenko was enough to tighten his chest, Pascha found himself grinning. 'Were you a journalist in a previous life?'

'You would know the answer to that yourself if you'd bothered to ask about my job,' she said tartly.

'I couldn't get a word in,' he said, raising his brow. 'You ask more questions than the old KGB.'

'That's because I'm incurably nosy.'

Picking up the wine bottle, he headed back to the table. 'Tell me about your job first and then I'll consider telling you about my relationship with Marat Plushenko.' He topped both their glasses up then deliberately tugged his chair out from under her feet and sat down.

For half a moment he thought she might put her feet back up and onto his lap.

For half a moment his skin tingled with anticipation.

What, he wondered, would she do if he were to lean a hand down and gather those pretty feet onto his lap…?

Emily took a sip of her wine. 'You want to know about my job?'

'I do.' It dawned on him that he wanted to know a lot more than that. Emily Richardson was the most intriguing person he'd met in a long time, maybe ever. A seemingly fearless woman without limits when it came to those she loved. 'You say you're in the fashion industry?'

'I'm an in-house designer for the House of Alexander.'

'Ah.' He nodded. 'You work for Hugo Alexander?'

'Yep.'

'All the pieces fall into place.' The House of Alexander was one of the UK's foremost fashion houses, famous for its theatrical, off-beat designs. Hugo Alexander's designs had captured the eye of fashion editors around the world and the imagination of the public. It was one of the fashion houses to buy on his radar.

'What, you mean the sewing machine and the rolls of fabric I brought here with me?'

'And all the fashion magazines littering your bedroom.' *And the way you dress*, he almost added. He couldn't think of a more suitable fashion house for her to work for. Not that she was dressed that way now. Since arriving on the island, all her theatricality had been stripped away.

'You could have been Sherlock Holmes in a previous life.'

Pascha didn't want to laugh. He didn't want to find Emily amusing but the truth, as he was rapidly finding, was that he did.

He couldn't remember the last time he'd found anyone fun to be around. It was not a trait he sought. Yes, many of the companies he'd bought over the years were run by flamboyant characters, but these were not people he mixed with on anything but a professional level.

'Do you remember that party you had when you first bought Bamber?' she asked.

'I remember it,' he said, surprised at her turn of the conversation. Throwing a getting-to-know-you party was something he always did when he bought a new company, wanting to meet his new staff on a more human footing than at their work stations.

'I was only dressed that way because I'd come straight from work—we'd just had a show and Hugo had steered us all in a gothic focus.'

He looked at her. 'So you don't normally dress as the Bride of Frankenstein?'

She laughed. 'Not to that extent. If I'd had the time, I would have changed into something a little more appropriate.'

'I thought you'd dressed that way deliberately.'

'If I'd had the time to change, I would have, but you know what fashion shows are like; the days just don't have enough hours in them.'

Pascha did know. When he'd bought his first fashion house he'd felt obliged to attend New York Fashion Week. He'd stayed for approximately one hour before boredom had set in and he'd made his escape. He'd felt the energy all the designers, make-up artists and all the other people involved had expelled, like a hive of creative bees working in perfect harmony. He could easily imagine Emily fitting into the hive with ease. 'How did you get into fashion?' he asked, curious to know.

'When I was a kid the only clothes available for little girls were "pretty" clothes and always in pink.' She pulled a face. 'I *hate* pink. I used to draw the clothes I wished I could wear. Eventually I badgered my mum enough that she taught me how to use her sewing machine.'

'Your mother was a seamstress?'

'If she hadn't had kids at such a young age, she probably would have been. Maybe if she'd lived a bit longer she might have gone on to do it.' She reached for her glass of wine and took a sip. Was it his imagination or was there a slight tremor in her hand?

Despite her threat to drink herself into a stupor, she'd had only the one rum and Coke, and had hardly touched her second glass of wine.

'Mum was so proud when I got the job with Hugo,' she said wistfully. A flash of pain crossed her face before she took another sip of her wine and then visibly braced herself, fixing a smile onto her face to say, 'Anyway, your turn.'

'My turn for what?'

'To tell me why you want to buy Plushenko's.'

Briefly Pascha considered batting the question away.

'It's not as if we've anything else we can do other than talk,' she pointed out, those meltingly gorgeous eyes fixing themselves on him, waiting.

His eyes dropped to her bare shoulder, his skin heating as he considered a different, far more pleasurable way in which they could pass the time…

He gave a brisk shake of his head.

He needed to get a handle on himself.

They might be getting along in the shelter better than he had hoped but it didn't change the facts. They had blackmailed each other. It was the only reason either of them was there.

'Marat Plushenko is my brother.'

Emily gave a low whistle. 'I didn't see that one coming. You're trying to buy your own brother's company? In secret?'

He sighed. There was little point in trying to cheat her with part of the story. 'We're not biological brothers. I never knew my biological father—he abandoned my mother before I was born. Marat's mother died when he was a toddler. Our parents married when I was eighteen months old and Marat five. Andrei adopted me, my mother adopted Marat.'

'Right…' She nodded slowly. 'So you were raised together as brothers?'

'Yes. We were raised together as brothers but Marat never accepted me as a brother.' He gave a rueful smile. 'He always hated me.'

A groove formed in her brow. 'Why?'

He rubbed his face. 'Marat never wanted anything to do with Plushenko's or with me—'

'Back up a minute,' she interrupted with a shake of her head. 'I've just got it—Andrei Plushenko is your adopted father, therefore you're part of the Plushenko dynasty?'

'A dynasty conveys a sense of longevity. Andrei founded the company.'

'I see.'

'Are you sure *you* weren't Sherlock Holmes in a previous life?'

She laughed. 'You were telling me about Marat,' she prodded.

'He set up a number of failed businesses—I think it was five in all. Eight years ago he decided he should join the family firm, except he wasn't prepared to work his way up and learn the business. He wanted to join at executive level.'

'You didn't agree with that?'

'No. To me, it was a ludicrous idea. I was happy for him to join us, almost as happy as Andrei was, but I thought he should learn the intricacies of the business first, just as I did.' He shook his head. 'Our father didn't see it like that. He was desperate for Marat to come aboard, would have given him anything he desired. It came to a head when I made the mistake of giving Andrei, our father, an ultimatum—if Marat joined the board, I would resign.'

'Did Andrei choose Marat?'

'Not in so many words.' He fixed suddenly bleak eyes on her. 'What he said was, "But, Pascha, he is my blood". I handed in my resignation the next day.'

'How did Andrei react to that?' Her voice was low, soft.

'He was very upset with my decision. My mother was too. But I was…' He almost said 'devastated' but stopped himself just in time. 'I was very angry about the situation, angry enough to change my name from Plushenko to my mother's maiden name. I'd joined the business straight from school, pushed for the international expansion, the new state-of-the-art workshop…'

He blew out a breath and shook his head as more memories assailed him. 'It took five years before I began to see things clearly but I never got the chance to make amends with Andrei— he died in his sleep three years ago. Marat took the reins. Since then, Plushenko's has gone to the dogs. Marat won't sell it to me so I formed RG Holdings as a front company, spent two years building it up and investing in companies so he wouldn't be suspicious.'

'*Why* does he hate you so much? You're his *brother.*'

His chest expanded to see her outrage on his behalf.

You're his brother.

He'd always wished that to be true.

'I don't know. I don't have any memories of life without him. But he was older when our parents married. He has memories of life without me.' He shook his head and raised his eyes to the ceiling before leaning back into his chair some more and placing his feet on the chair beside her.

'Maybe a more pertinent question to ask is why I'm telling you any of this.'

Her gaze still resting on him, she raised a shoulder in a rueful shrug, the expression on her face indicating she didn't know the answer to that any more than he did.

He breathed heavily and got to his feet. 'More wine?' As a rule, he didn't drink much alcohol, too conscious of the effects it had on the body. Tonight, he was prepared to make an exception.

She covered her glass with her hand. 'Not for me, thank you.'

'Have you abandoned your idea of drinking yourself into a stupor?' he asked lightly.

'I'd only get really giggly and annoying, and we both know I'm annoying enough as it is,' she replied, her light tone matching his.

'In that case, how about I get you a glass of milk?'

She laughed but her eyes remained troubled. 'I might take you up on that later. Right now, I think I need a shower. My hair is still full of sea salt.'

'Okay, well, while you do that I'm going to check in with my lawyer.' He didn't hold out much hope that his battery would last long but he needed something to distract him.

Sharing his past did not come easily to him, but then he'd never found himself in this kind of situation before, where talking really was the only way of passing the time. The only way apart from the obvious, that was, which categorically could not happen. It just couldn't.

No matter how tempting he found her: a bundle of sin with porcelain skin and ebony hair.

CHAPTER SEVEN

EMILY SPENT A long time in the shower, clearing her muddled thoughts.

Pascha Virshilas was the enemy. She had to remember that.

But she was hanging on to her hate by the tips of her fingers, the threads she'd gripped her loathing onto loosening to such an extent she couldn't keep a proper hold on them.

Simply enjoying his company felt like stepping into enemy territory. This was the man who hadn't given her recently widowed father the chance to defend himself before suspending him without pay; the man who'd left her father to flounder in a pit of despair rather than start the investigation which would have cleared his name. This was the man who had left her father to rot.

He'd looked out for *her,* though.

Donning a knee-length black dress—when

had her wardrobe become so *dark*? She really needed to inject some more colour into it—she went back into the main part of the shelter and found Pascha sitting on the sofa reading a book.

'I thought there wasn't any form of entertainment here,' she said mock-accusingly.

He held the book up. 'I'm afraid all the reading material in here is in Russian.'

'Never mind.' She wandered past him and over to the kitchen.

She needed something to do, something to keep her mind occupied so it wouldn't be so full of *him*.

'If I'd known I would be having an English guest, I would have arranged for some books of your own language to be stocked.'

'I'm hardly your guest, though, am I?' She said it for her own benefit as well as his—a reminder to them both.

He put his book down and raised a brow. 'While you are on this island, you are my guest and you will be treated as such.'

It was on the tip of her tongue to rebuke him, to point out that guests were generally allowed to communicate with the outside world. And that, oh, as a rule, guests weren't usually forced on to their host's island.

For once she kept her tongue still.

They both knew the facts. There was little point rehashing them.

They had a long night ahead of them. Better to try and sustain the strange kind of harmony they'd managed to establish.

As long as she continued to keep her guard up, she would be fine.

Rooting round the kitchenette for something to do, she found a large tub of vanilla ice-cream in the freezer. There was nothing better than ice-cream to aid harmony.

'Do you want some?' she asked, holding it up for him.

'Sure,' he replied with a shrug, closing his book and placing it on the arm of the sofa.

Grabbing two spoons, she took it over to the table.

Pascha pulled out the chair opposite her and nodded at the tub. 'No bowls?'

'Saves washing up.'

'It'll melt.'

'No, it won't. I guarantee that in ten minutes it

will all be gone.' She might not have been able to manage much of her dinner, but ice-cream… now, *that* she could happily eat, however fraught her emotions. 'If you want a bowl, help yourself.'

Rolling his eyes, he got himself a bowl, sat down and methodically scooped some ice-cream into it.

'Is that all you're having?' she asked with incredulity. He'd only put two scoops into his bowl.

He quelled her with a look. 'It's hardly a healthy food.'

'It's ice-cream. It's not supposed to be healthy. It's supposed to be comforting.'

'I'll be sure to tell my arteries that.'

They ate in silence but, unlike over dinner, this silence didn't have an uncomfortable edge to it. Probably because no one could be uncomfortable whilst eating divine vanilla ice-cream. The sweetness was soothing.

While they ate, Pascha checked his phone.

'Did you manage to get hold of your lawyer?' she asked.

'Just. The battery died after a couple of minutes.' He gave it a shake, as if hoping it would miraculously charge itself.

'You do realise you're torturing yourself by checking it?' she said.

He pursed his lips. 'It's pointless, I know. I just find it incredibly frustrating.'

'Have some more ice-cream.'

'Will that help?' he asked mockingly.

'Nope. But it will make the frustration taste a bit sweeter.' To make her point, she put a delicious spoonful into her mouth.

His lips twitched.

She grinned to see him scoop a little more into his bowl, but only a little. 'Have you always been a control freak?'

His eyes narrowed a touch. 'I like to control the environment in which I live,' he answered slowly.

'We all do that to an extent,' she agreed. 'But you seem to be quite extreme about it.'

He put his spoon down. 'I had leukaemia as a child,' he said simply.

Startled, Emily felt her eyes widen.

He'd had *leukaemia*…?

'Being so close to death so young…' He raised a shoulder. 'It shapes you. It shaped me.'

'I don't know what to say,' she said starkly. 'Are you okay now? I mean…'

'I know what you mean and, yes, I am in good health.' He hadn't escaped unscathed, though, Pascha reflected with a trace of bitterness. Five years of chemotherapy and all the other associated treatments had given him a future but had also come with one particular cost, a cost that no amount of money could ever fix.

'But I do not take my good health for granted. I freely admit I like to take control of my life, but when you have spent five of your formative years with no control over your body or your treatment, and no control over how it affects those you love…' He shook his head and scraped out the last of the ice-cream in his bowl. 'Now I am in control. Just me. To use business jargon, I will not outsource it.'

Emily had stopped eating, her spoon held in mid-air. 'I'm so sorry.' She shook her head, a dazed expression on her face. 'That must have been awful for you. Terrifying. And your poor parents. It doesn't bear thinking about, does it? It's hard enough watching your parents suffer but when it comes to your own child…' Her words tailed off and she seemed to give herself a mental shake, sticking her spoon back into the tub.

'Yes, it was hard for them,' he agreed, his voice dropping, his mind wandering back to a time when his mother had seemingly aged overnight. One minute she'd been a young mother with an easy laugh, the next a middle-aged woman with lines on her face.

The memories had the power to lance his guts.

His mind drifted back to those—literally—dark days, when they'd been so poor his parents could only afford to heat his bedroom. That had been when Marat's disdain for his younger, adopted brother had turned ugly. How clearly he recalled Marat whispering to him when their parents had been out of earshot, 'Why don't you just die and save us all this trouble, Cuckoo?' Pascha might have been only seven years old but he'd known his brother meant it.

'Cuckoo': Marat's secret nickname for him.

He looked down at his empty bowl.

To hell with it.

He could allow himself one night of sweetness.

He stuck his spoon into the tub and ate straight from it.

Something flickered in Emily's eyes as she did

the same, their spoons clashing as they dived into the tub a second time.

The flickering darkened and swirled, their eyes locked.

She really was incredibly beautiful. And incredibly easy to talk to.

With a stab, he realised he'd shared more of his past with her this evening than he had ever done with anyone. His childhood illness was history, not something he talked about.

He looked at his watch. 'Half an hour.'

A groove he was starting to recognise formed on her brow. 'Half an hour...?'

'That's how long it's taken us to finish this tub of ice-cream. You said ten minutes.'

'Too much talking, not enough eating. And it's not finished.' She yanked the tub up and peered into it. 'There's at least a spoonful left.'

'You finish it.'

'How very magnanimous.'

He watched as she seemingly scraped out every last drop of the by now melted remnants.

His blood thickened at witnessing her pink tongue dart out to lick the spoon.

Mentally taking a deep breath, he got to his

feet. Tonight he was also going to say to hell with his strict diet and limited alcohol consumption. 'How about we open another bottle of wine?'

'Why not?' she agreed, pushing the tub away from her. 'It's more exciting than milk.' She placed a hand on her middle. 'Do you think it's any good for stomach-ache?'

Why did that action automatically make him think of a pregnant woman rubbing her swollen bump?

He blinked the image away, unsettled at the imagery.

'Has someone eaten too much ice-cream?'

'Mmm…maybe,' she said, elongating the first syllable.

'I hate to say I told you so…'

She pulled a face. 'I know, I know, too much ice-cream is unhealthy. That didn't stop you from eating half of it.'

'Not quite half,' he said with a wry smile, pushing his chair back. He'd eaten more ice-cream in one sitting than he'd consumed in the past decade.

Emily was right. It made bitterness much easier to swallow.

Or was it that she was such a good listener that it made it easier to spill the secrets of his past?

When he sat back down with the bottle and two clean glasses, she leaned forward and rested her chin on her hands. 'Being stuck in here with me must be a nightmare for you. First the engine of the yacht breaking, then the storm… It must be driving you mad, all these things occurring that are out of your control.'

He laughed. 'I'm coping.' To his surprise, he realised, he was coping remarkably well.

Under normal circumstances, an event like this would elicit a vigorous amount of pacing the room, waiting for the danger of the storm to pass. But instead he was content to sit back, relax and just…talk.

When had he ever taken the time just to *talk*?

No wonder he wasn't going mad when he had Emily to distract him, something she managed to do effortlessly.

He gripped the stem of his glass, fighting a sudden compulsion to reach over and touch her hair. She'd left it loose. Her curls had dried since her shower, a mass of long ebony ringlets springing here, there and everywhere.

What did that gorgeous hair smell of? he wondered. What, he wondered, would she do if he were to capture one of the locks and wind it around his finger?

Every sinew in his body tightened.

He took a large swallow of his wine, watching as she reached for her glass and did likewise, running a finger over the flesh of her bottom lip to wipe a drop away.

He took another swallow and forced a smile at her questioning look.

He wished there was another tub of ice-cream in the freezer. Maybe he could spoon it straight onto his lap and kill the heat simmering in him.

Emily sat curled up in the armchair she'd dragged over to the wall so she could peer out of the porthole-like window. Only the dim glow from the outside lights enabled her to see the trees bending under the assault of the wind. Rain lashed down like a sheet, more powerful than anything she'd ever witnessed.

She shivered.

'Are you cold?'

She shook her head, keeping her face pressed to the window.

'I'll get you a blanket.'

'I'm not cold.' It was looking at the storm that had made her shiver. All the same, when Pascha gave her the soft fleece blanket, she wrapped it around her shoulders with gratitude, murmuring her thanks.

By the time they'd finished their wine, the atmosphere between them had shifted. A growing charge had sent her away from the dining table to where she was now, holed up by the window.

If she couldn't look at him, she couldn't notice how utterly gorgeous he was.

If she couldn't talk to him, she couldn't feel the richness of his voice seeping through her veins…

How long would the storm go on for? It seemed interminable.

They'd been in the shelter for six hours. The time was really stretching now, and so was the tension brewing between them. She could feel it with every breath. And what made it worse was that she knew he felt it too.

She didn't know much about leukaemia other than that survival rates had improved dramatically in recent years. How old was he? Thirty-four? When he'd had it, the survival rates had been dire. The battle would have been immense. She kept imagining the small child he'd been and the desperate worry of his parents. She wanted to travel back to the past and hug that small child.

It explained so much about him.

For the first time, she tried to think from his point of view. There he was, pouring all his energy into buying the firm his adored adopted father had founded, having to do it amidst the highest secrecy, when he'd learned a sum of money had gone missing on a senior executive's watch. He hardly knew this employee. The sum was significant by any normal person's standards, but to a billionaire it wasn't significant enough to warrant an immediate investigation, not when priorities lay elsewhere.

Twirling a curl absently around her finger, Emily sighed. However much she might disagree with his methods, she understood the reasons.

If only she wasn't so aware of him. Her attention might be firmly fixed on what was going on outside but still she sensed every move he made.

He was back on the sofa, his nose buried in his book.

Even if there had been a book in English she wouldn't have been able to concentrate. There was too much energy racing through her veins. More than that, she was too consumed with *him* to concentrate properly on anything.

She heard every page he turned. She knew every time he ran his fingers through his hair. She knew when he stretched his long legs out.

After another hour of silence had passed, during which the storm hadn't abated at all, she heard him close his book.

'I need to get some sleep,' he said. 'You can have the bed. I'll take the sofa.'

'Don't worry about it—I'm a night owl. You take the bed. I'm happy watching the storm.' Before he could open his mouth to argue, she turned her head and threw him a wry smile. 'I'm half your size and probably need half the sleep you do. It's more logical for me to take the sofa.'

Pascha wanted to argue with her but, studying Emily's expression, he could see she didn't look remotely tired.

He wasn't tired either.

His body clock, usually so good at regulating his sleeping patterns, appeared to have gone on strike.

But he had to sleep—at least had to try to—even if Emily *was* sitting mere feet away from him.

'If the sofa is too uncomfortable, feel free to join me in the bed,' he said in as casual a tone as he could muster. 'You have nothing to fear from me.'

His veins thickened anew at the thought of her climbing in beside him, her sweet scent inches from him, close enough for him to reach a hand out, touch her skin and discover for himself if it was as silky as it seemed. Close enough to discover for himself exactly what her glorious hair smelled like.

With iron will, he forced the torrent of desire away.

'I know.' She turned her face back to the window before he could read what was written on it.

After brushing his teeth, he poured himself a glass of water and padded around the shelter turning off all the lights bar the small lamp near where Emily sat curled like a cat.

Her concentration was firmly focussed on the storm outside, yet he could feel her awareness of him as keenly as he felt his own awareness of her.

Did she realise she'd been twirling that same curl round her finger for the past hour?

He stripped to his boxers and slid under the covers. Usually he slept nude but tonight he felt it more appropriate to wear something. He didn't want her feeling uncomfortable with him. 'Goodnight, Emily.'

She didn't look at him. 'Night.'

His eyes wouldn't close. Try as he might, he couldn't stop his mind drifting into what would happen if she *did* join him in the bed. He didn't think he'd ever felt the blood running through his veins so keenly, a thick desire that, if he'd been alone, he'd be able to do something about. If he'd been with any other woman, he'd have been able to do something about it too. Since making his fortune, he'd never been rebuffed by a woman. But he'd never felt a woman's disinterest in his money as keenly as he did with Emily. His wealth meant nothing to her.

She was only here on Aliana Island with him, in a storm shelter, out of sufferance.

No, he corrected himself. She was here out of love. Love for her father.

She was also a thief, he reminded himself. However good her intentions, she'd stolen her father's pass key, incited someone into giving her the code—he would find out who as soon as he returned to the UK—and had intended to steal every scrap of data from his hard drive. If he hadn't returned earlier from Milan than intended, she would have got away with it.

And yet…

Her actions had been born out of desperation. Born out of love.

As sleep continued to elude him, he cursed that he hadn't sent her to the staff shelter. Forget all his good reasons not to have done; for the amount he paid them, his staff could have put up with Emily for one night. Sleep was an essential function of his life. He'd never forgotten the words of his doctors when he'd been a child. *Sleep will help you get better,* they'd told him. And he *had* got better. He'd recovered. He'd beaten the odds and he'd survived.

He heard movement—Emily quietly making herself a hot drink before settling back on the armchair.

Pascha willed sleep to come quickly.

CHAPTER EIGHT

SLEEP DIDN'T COME. Time dragged ever more slowly. But Pascha must have drifted off at some point, for one minute Emily was there and the next she was gone.

Rubbing his eyes, he sat up. The armchair she'd been sitting in was empty. The small lamp still glowed.

He checked his watch and saw it was three a.m.

He looked through the porthole. It appeared the worst of the storm was over. The trees still swayed but the rain had stopped.

Stopping only to pull on a pair of shorts, he turned the handle. The door was unlocked. Stepping outside, he found her huddled up in the fleece blanket on the bench in front of the shelter.

The chill of the breeze hit him immediately. Not all the storm clouds had disappeared but right above Aliana Island they had cleared enough to reveal a black night sky alight with stars.

She turned her face to him. Under the glow of the outside light he could see her desolation.

'It's three o'clock,' he said gently, crouching down to her height, noting that she'd taken the padded mats off the dining table chairs and placed them along the bench to sit on.

She nodded, blinking rapidly. She cleared her throat. 'I needed some air. I'll come back in if the wind picks up any more.'

She isn't a child, he reminded himself. If she wanted to sit out in the cold wind, then that was her business. But the look on her face reminded him of a child. Emily looked lost.

He sat next to her, thankful for the mats she'd placed on the bench.

At first she didn't acknowledge him, simply kept her deadened gaze on the starry sky.

After long moments of silence, she opened her mouth. 'When I was a little girl, my mum told me the stars were our dead ancestors looking down on us.'

'That's a nice thing to believe,' he answered carefully.

'I want it to be true. I want to believe she's up there looking over us all.' She hugged the blanket tighter around herself. 'You know you asked me why I went into fashion?'

He nodded, a pointless gesture with her eyes still staring upwards.

'It was because of her. It was a way to spend time with her, just me. She loved us all but so much of her time was spent managing Dad's depression and trying to limit its impact on me and James that sometimes it was hard to get her to myself. We'd hole ourselves up in her study and design and make our own clothing. I kept trying to talk her into going to my old fashion college as a mature student, but she kept putting it off, saying she would do it one day. And now it's too late. She'll never do it. All the dreams she had…all gone.'

'When did she die?'

'Three months ago.'

The jolt this information gave him felt like a physical blow.

Three months?

That meant Malcolm Richardson had lost his wife only weeks before the money had gone missing…

He lost his train of thought when he felt her

slump beside him, saw her drop forward to wrap her arms around her knees and bury her face.

For too long he stared at her shaking body before placing a hand on her back.

She shuddered. He thought she was going to shrug off his ineffectual attempt at comfort; instead she twisted into him, placing her head on his chest as she sobbed, her tears falling onto his naked skin.

Pascha didn't think he'd ever felt as inadequate as he did at that moment. All he could do was stroke her hair with the palm of his hand, his guts a tangled knot.

His mind raced, a confusion of thoughts he couldn't begin to decipher.

Only three months…

'I miss her so badly.' Emily spoke in gasps, her breaths warming his stomach. 'I can't believe she's gone. I just want her back.'

What could he say? Nothing.

'When she was diagnosed we knew she wouldn't have long but it happened so *quickly*. Seven months. That's all we had—that's all *she* had. Seven months. All the time in the world would never have been enough.'

It was as if a floodgate had opened. Emily's anguish spilled out, unable to be contained.

'What happened to her?' he asked quietly, nestling his hand into her hair and cradling her scalp protectively.

It took a few attempts for her to get the words out. 'She had Progressive Bulbar Palsy.'

'What's that?'

'A form of motor neurone disease. Very aggressive. So cruel….' Her words tailed away.

'Is that why you took all that time off work?' he asked, his stomach clenching. He'd assumed it had all been tied to her father's recent mental breakdown; he'd had no idea it stretched back so long.

She rocked into him. 'I had to be there. So little time.' Emily couldn't speak any more, her vocal cords choked by her grief.

Since the diagnosis, Emily had worked on autopilot, on the go all the time, never sitting still long enough actually to face what was happening to her mother full-on. It had been the same when she'd died.

She hadn't cried since the funeral, too worried

about her father to grieve for the woman they'd all adored.

'Let me ask you something.' Pascha spoke in a gentle tone that soothed her as much as the tender movements of his hand in her hair, massaging her scalp. 'When your mother died, did she know how much you loved her?'

She tilted her face to look at him. His face was crinkled, his eyes a litany of emotion. She nodded in response, still unable to speak.

'Then you did have enough time, *milaya moya.*' His finger brushed against her cheek, his grey eyes swirling with emotion. 'I know it doesn't feel like you did and you're right—all the time in the world would never have been enough. But for your mother to go to her grave knowing how much you all loved her is the greatest gift you could have given her. For that, you were blessed with all the time you needed.'

Even through the pain of her grief, Emily could feel the sorrow beneath the empathetic tone of his words. Her hand moved on its own accord to touch his face. Dark stubble had slowly spread along his jawline throughout the evening, a roughness to the touch that felt impossibly comforting.

She shifted a little, moving her face up his chest so her cheek rested on his shoulder. 'Are you thinking of your father?'

His jaw clenched but he nodded. 'I never got the chance to say goodbye or to—' He cut his own words off, tilting his head back to look at the sky thickening with clouds once again. 'I never told him how much he meant to me.'

'I'm sorry,' she whispered.

He looked back down at her, his usually composed features raw.

Emily had been there at the end, holding her mother's hand when she'd slipped away. They'd all been there. It was a comfort knowing her mum had been with the people she loved most when the end had come, that she hadn't left this life alone.

All Pascha had was regrets. She could feel them as keenly as she felt their mutual sorrow.

She had no idea how long they sat there gazing at each other, his hand nestled in her hair, her fingertips tracing his stubbly jawline.

She wanted to kiss him. She wanted to feel

those wide, firm lips upon hers and learn for herself what they'd feel like upon her mouth. And from the deepening of Pascha's breath and the growing intensity in his eyes she could tell that he wanted it too.

His head dipped at the same moment she raised her chin, their lips coming together in a whisper of movement. He exhaled at the same moment she expelled the breath she hadn't realised she'd been holding and, inhaling again, she breathed him in, a dark, masculine essence that filled her with such deep longing.

She pulled back to stare at him, recognising the same puzzlement in his own stare as she knew must be in hers.

But then their lips came together again, his strong arms enveloped her and he was kissing her properly, his tongue sweeping into her mouth, filling her senses with his exotic taste.

As if they had free will, her arms wrapped around his broad shoulders and she pressed her hands to his skin. It was smoother to the touch than she could ever have imagined and she traced her fingers over it in circles.

The deeper his kisses, the more she wanted,

soaking in as much of his taste and touch as she could consume.

Time slipped away, the world shrinking just to them, a mesh of hungry lips and tongues devouring each other.

His hand swept down her back to clasp her thigh over the restriction of the blanket she was nestled in.

Her blanket.

For the first time, she considered how cold he must be in the whipping wind.

While she was all snuggled up in the fleece blanket, Pascha was sat in nothing but a pair of shorts.

It wasn't just the wind lashing around them either; the rain had started again, not as fierce as earlier but picking up quickly, big, fat droplets of it.

'We should go back inside before we get pneumonia,' she said, disentangling her arms from around him, swallowing hard.

Pascha hadn't noticed the rain. He'd stopped feeling the cold.

One kiss and he'd forgotten himself.

He'd forgotten his health.

For the first time since the age of five, he didn't care.

How the hell had that happened?

Emily slipped off his lap—when had she climbed onto it?—and got back to her feet in such an unsteady fashion he grabbed her arm to stop her falling.

'Thanks,' she muttered, stepping back with wide, pained eyes before disappearing back into the shelter.

Pausing only to collect the seat covers on the bench, he followed her in, locking the door behind him.

She'd disappeared into the bathroom. He took the moment of solitude to inhale deeply and calm his racing thoughts.

Never had he felt desire so strong.

Or so wrong.

To allow anything more than a kiss to develop between them was to take the first steps on the road to madness.

Emily was nothing like the women he usually entertained for his gratification. She was all too real. All too human. And she was vulnerable.

But his good intentions died when she reappeared from the bathroom, a white towel wrapped around her, accentuating her feminine curves.

All the moisture left his mouth. All the words he'd planned to say left with it.

She passed him a hand-towel with which to dry himself. Wordlessly he accepted it, rubbing it over his hair and face.

She closed the gap between them and placed a hand on his chest. The heat from her skin warmed him more than any fire ever could have.

Slowly Emily traced her fingers over him. It was every bit as beautiful as the tantalising glimpse she'd caught on the veranda had promised, his chest hard and golden, the dark hairs covering it soft.

His chest rose, as if he were struggling for breath. He caught her wrist. 'Emily, I do not want to take advantage of the situation.'

She could see the pain on his face as he spoke the words. As she closed the final gap between them, pressing herself so her mouth was against his collarbone, she could feel the strength of his erection through his shorts, a movement that sent a bloom of heat straight between her thighs. 'You might not want to take advantage of the situation, but *I* do,' she whispered.

How could she not? The whole day felt like a dream. So many emotions had been churned up, so much desire. And right then it was the desire that burned the strongest, enough to drive out all the other emotions living within her, all her fears.

Stepping back, she tugged at her towel and let it fall to the floor, watching as his eyes widened, the grey darkening.

It was her turn for eyes to widen when a strong hand clasped her waist and wrenched her to him. Before she had time to breathe, Pascha's hot mouth had found hers, his hold on her the only thing keeping her boneless legs upright.

She wound her arms around his neck and clung to him, kissing him back with everything she had, her tongue winding around his, dancing a tune she never wanted to end.

When Emily had been a child she had always adored watching couples kissing on the television and had eagerly anticipated her own first kiss. In her head, she'd envisaged it would be just like the movies and would send her into a frenzy on the spot. Needless to say, her first kiss had been a disappointment. It was nothing she could put her finger on but kissing had never sent the shockwaves through her that she had always secretly hoped for.

She could kiss Pascha for a lifetime. His kisses were everything she had yearned for and more, sending ripples of pleasure careering through her veins and tingles of electricity zipping through her skin. His kisses were perfect.

She wanted to cry out when he broke away and stepped back. Without any preamble, he slid his shorts off and kicked them away.

He stood before her, fully erect.

Her breath caught in her throat. He was beautiful in every way.

He reached out a hand and placed it on her breast, simply resting it there, his fingers gently cupping the swollen skin. Fresh desire shot through her and she sucked in a breath, fighting the urge to close her eyes. She wanted to see everything. She wanted to feel everything. Beneath his touch, her nipples puckered and hardened and she arched slightly into him, her mouth filling with moisture, the heat between her legs growing and bubbling.

Mirroring his movement, she splayed a hand on his chest and tugged the silky hair between her fingers, adoring the feel of his warm skin beneath her touch, the hard satin-smoothness of it.

His free hand clasped her neck and began a lazy trail over her collarbone and down past her breasts. Down his fingers trailed, skimming lightly over her belly before slipping further down still.

A gasp escaped her throat and their eyes widened, mirroring each other. Pascha was dumbfounded. He'd known she wanted him but he'd had no idea how deeply her desire ran or how closely it matched his own throbbing need.

Jaw clenched, he fought to keep his head, to keep some basic control.

Snaking one hand around her waist, he used the other to capture her chin and gaze deeply into those mesmerising eyes, the flicker of fire burning from them; they were like precious jewels. Slowly he brought his mouth down and kissed her, her lips parting at the first touch as they forged back together in a fury that threatened to unravel his restraint.

Emily's fingers skimmed up his chest and her

hands hooked around his neck. She pressed into him, moving against his erection, her breasts crushed against him.

Unable to bear the thought of breaking contact with her luscious soft flesh, Pascha half-dragged and half-carried Emily to the bed. There, they fell onto it in a heap, her melodious easy laughter like music.

He gazed in wonder, taking in all the features of her face, from the large brown eyes that glowed with sensuous promise to the heart-shaped lips curved in a half-shy, half-wanton smile. He took in the faint smattering of freckles the sun had exposed on her delicate skin and wondered if a more beautiful woman existed—but, no; in his eyes, that would be impossible. Perfection was lying beneath him hooking an impatient arm around his neck and tugging his head down to capture his lips in a deeply passionate kiss that made his blood burn into a fever.

'You're beautiful,' he whispered before burying his face in her neck and kissing his way down to her perfectly ripe breasts.

Moving his lips over each of them in turn, his need deepening with every second, he forced his mind to detach. He was close to the edge. He could feel it.

Reluctantly he abandoned the softness of her breasts and snaked his way down her body, smiling at her jolt as he moved lower. How many more of her secrets were there to uncover?

Casting his head lower still, over her dark, downy hair, he felt her body tense slightly when he gently prised her thighs apart and laid between her parted legs. Gazing up at her through hooded eyes, he was gratified to see her head thrown back, her breathing shallow through her parted lips.

He dipped his head, his tongue immediately homing in on the nub of her pleasure. She tasted wonderful, of musky, sexy woman. Her breathy, responsive whimpers only served to fire him further, and when her fingers clasped his hair, and she raised her buttocks and writhed beneath him, he feared his own peak was nearing.

And then he felt her stiffen, her whole body lifting from the mattress, her fingers digging into his scalp as her orgasm rippled through her.

The white light flickering behind Emily's eyelids slowly dispersed. The deep pulses flowing through her body dissolved into a trillion tiny tingles that burrowed from the tips of her toes all the way up to her scalp. Dazed, she lifted her head up and opened her eyes. Pascha's chin now rested on her abdomen and he was gazing at her with something akin to wonder.

Wordlessly he crawled up the length of her body until he was on top of her, his nose touching hers. Their lips came together and she wrapped her arms around him, the bodies pressed together so tightly it was impossible to know where she began and he ended.

A whimper of panic flew from her mouth when he pulled—ripped—away from their embrace.

Placing a tender finger to her lips, he smiled crookedly. 'I must get some protection.'

She twitched a nod and attempted a smile in return. As she watched his retreating figure head to the bathroom, she took deep breaths, trying desperately to contain the ragged beat of her heart.

Pascha was back by her side in less than thirty seconds yet those beats seemed interminably long.

Her gaze moved to the square silver packet in his hand.

He gathered a handful of curls and moved them aside to place a solitary kiss on her neck. Looking back at her, his eyes burned, sparkles flying into her and liquefying her core all over again. 'Do you want to put it on?'

But Emily's hand was shaking. It was nothing but anticipation, she frantically told herself. She was a twenty-first-century woman.

So why, then, did she suddenly feel so vulnerable?

She wanted this more than she had wanted anything in her life. And that was terrifying.

He leaned forward and kissed her, a kiss full of passion and hunger, a kiss that blew everything else from her mind. She slipped a hand down his arm and caught hold of his fingers. Together, their lips still locked, they rolled the condom on. Done, Pascha smoothly manoeuvred her onto her back and pushed her legs apart, his big hands stroking her thighs before curving up her sides, up the sides of her breasts, up to her neck, before resting on the pillow either side of her head.

Her lips suddenly cold as he broke the kiss, Emily's eyes fluttered open and locked onto his.

The sensation of drowning flooded her. She could feel the strong thud of his heart hammering against his chest, reverberating through her skin and burrowing through her ribcage to match the unsteady tempo of her own.

Pascha placed his lips on her mouth, just a light pressure, his breath flowing into her pores and filling her mouth with sweet heat and moisture. Every nerve-ending in her body burned, demanding his possession, and when he finally entered her she had no control over the high-pitched moan that flew from her mouth.

Keeping her eyes wide open, she raised a hand to his cheek, savouring the feel of him inside her, filling her completely.

His movements were torturously controlled as he began to move, his kisses intensifying as he deepened the penetration, their bodies fusing into one pulsating, rhythmic mass.

Emily was helpless in his arms, unable to do anything but clasp tight to him and repeat his name over and over in a desperate voice that was not her own, taking every ounce of the pleasure he was bestowing. Pascha began to drive harder and faster into her and still all she could do was cling to him, nothing but willing putty in his hands until, finally, the tension tightening in her core exploded. Waves of pulsating ripples tore through her into a crescendo of colour that blinded her in its brilliance.

Dimly she was aware of his movements becoming more frantic, his groans deepening until he gave one last powerful thrust and crashed on top of her.

For long minutes her head was nothing but mist. Pascha's breath was hot on her neck. Her fingers idly caressed his scalp and the nape of his neck, her eyes locked on the ceiling.

As the mist began to clear and the sensations absorbing her body started to lessen, the world came back into focus. But it was all wrong. It was nothing she could put her finger on; it was like looking at the world through a different lens, a tiny shift in the spectrum.

But that tiny shift was enough to tell her she would never be the same again.

CHAPTER NINE

THE STORM HAD cleared when Emily awoke, a beam of light pouring through the small porthole.

Pascha's side of the bed was empty.

She looked at her watch. It was only eight a.m. and she'd only had minimal sleep but it had been enough to see her through what she already knew was going to be a long day.

The bathroom was empty. She dived inside and locked the door. A minute later she stood under the steady stream of the shower. For an age she did nothing other than let the hot water pour over her body. The same body that had woken barely two hours before to make love to him all over again.

She could still feel the press of his lips to hers…

She could still taste him…

A flush swept through her that had nothing to do with the steam of the shower.

Every atom of her body danced with an energy she had never experienced before.

But mixed with the dancing was a deep feeling of dread right in the base of her stomach, a warning that she had made what could be the biggest mistake of her life.

However much she wanted to, she couldn't hide in the shower for the rest of her life. She had to face him under the light of day sooner or later.

Dressing in a clean black bikini and a sheer viridian-green sarong, she made herself a cup of tea then opened the door of the shelter.

The early heat of the day hit her immediately, warming her skin. She breathed it in, eyeing her surroundings, looking at the destruction from the night before. Dozens of trees had been felled, the clearing in front of the shelter littered with leaves and snapped-off branches. The shelter appeared to have escaped unscathed. She doubted the lodge had got off so lightly.

There was no sign of Pascha.

She sat back on the same bench from the night before; it was bone-dry, as if the rain had never lashed it. In the daylight she saw it had been welded to the concrete beneath it, a sign of Pascha having taken no chances, not even with a bench. The thought brought a wry smile to her lips.

The man thought of everything.

Inhaling deeply, she looked around. All the stars had gone; the sky was bright and cloudless. For the first time she was able to appreciate the view, a vista even more spectacular than the one from her veranda. In the distance were the neighbouring islands cresting out of the calm, sparkling ocean. She hoped they hadn't suffered too much in the storm.

She sensed rather than heard movement. Holding her breath, she waited as Pascha sat next to her, keeping a respectable distance between them. Her heart hammered painfully beneath her ribs.

'What's the damage?' she asked. At least her vocal cords worked. That was something.

'I haven't been to the lodge yet. I was waiting for you to wake.'

She supposed this was her cue to get to her feet and get her stuff together.

Closing her eyes briefly to brace herself, she fixed a nonchalant look on her face and turned her head to look at him.

At some point that morning he'd shaved. His hair had resumed its usual immaculate state. Somehow the chinos and polo shirt he'd changed into were properly pressed.

An ache bloomed low in her abdomen, climbing all the way up to tighten in her chest.

Pascha stared at the beautiful face he'd woken up to.

He'd had possibly the worst sleep of his life but also, somehow, the best. He'd listened in the dark as Emily's breathing had deepened and slowed into a regular drawn-out beat. At one point she'd turned in her sleep, her face just inches from his own. He'd gazed at her lips, barely visible in the darkness, and had pressed the lightest of kisses to them. His body hardened at the memory of her taste, a sultry sweetness that fired his loins anew.

Her hair smelt like raspberries.

Everything inside him tightened.

Mingling with his desire was guilt. It plagued him.

If he'd known Malcolm Richardson's wife had

died only a few weeks before the money had disappeared, he would have handled the matter differently. He wouldn't have suspended him summarily without giving him a chance to put his side across. He would have been far gentler in his approach.

Pascha had been so wrapped up in the Plushenko deal that he'd put everything else on the back burner, including the internal investigation into the missing money. So wrapped up had he been that not one employee who knew Malcolm Richardson had dared tell him of his recent widowhood.

He put himself in Emily's shoes. If it had been Andrei accused of stealing money…

He would have done anything to clear his name. He would have believed in his father's innocence every bit as fiercely as Emily believed in Malcolm's.

'I'm sorry.'

A groove appeared in her brow that he wanted to smooth away. 'I should have known your father had been so recently widowed.'

Her gaze remained steady but something flickered. 'Yes; yes, you should have.'

He sighed heavily. 'I really am very sorry. I wish I'd known about your mother. I would have handled things a lot differently if I had.'

She nodded and sank her teeth into her lips before saying, 'Please, do me a favour and clear his name. I know you're going to drop the suspension and everything, but he still needs to be cleared properly for his peace of mind. I swear he never took that money.'

'I will get it prioritised.'

'Thank you.' Her eyes held his, something swirling in them that disappeared before he could read it, and she straightened, as if giving herself a mental shake-down.

'I'll get my stuff together and we can go back to the lodge.' She didn't wait for his response before disappearing back into the shelter.

'What's that place?' Emily asked shortly after they started the walk back to the lodge, spotting a pretty concrete hut through the foliage.

'One of the guest shelters.'

'Like the one we stayed in?' She mentally applauded her outward nonchalance. So long as she kept the conversation impersonal she would be fine. Her stomach felt all knotted and twisted, though, and she inhaled deeply, trying to loosen all the constrictions within her.

She was reading too much into her jumbled emotions. So they'd made love; that didn't have to mean anything. People made love all the time. Well, other people did.

She'd been single for too long, that was her problem. Her emotional state made her vulnerable too. It was no wonder her heart raced when she was around him.

'It's identical. There are three of them for guests to shelter in if a storm hits so they can retain their privacy.'

'Why didn't you put me in one?'

He turned his head to look at her. 'I didn't want you sitting through that storm alone.'

The warm glow his words evoked in her made her feel flustered.

Why, oh why couldn't he be the evil monster she'd assumed him to be at the beginning?

But then, if he had been that evil monster, she would never have made love to him. She would never have clung to him for support and comfort when her grief had threatened to drown her with its strength.

The further down the trail they went, the more the wreckage from the storm became apparent. The majority of the pathway was covered with felled trees, branches and tiny twigs sharp enough to cut into flesh. Pascha enfolded her hand in his, helping her clear it all, his care expanding her heart so much it threatened to smother her lungs and stop them working.

The main house of the lodge appeared to have survived the storm without any damage. It was lucky. Devastation abounded everywhere else.

Half of the roof was missing from the hut where all the game paraphernalia was stored, a yellow cordon already erected around it. A tree had fallen onto the roof of the dining hut and had cut straight through it like a hot knife slicing through butter. Everywhere the eye could see lay scattered debris.

But it was at the jetty that the real destruction had occurred. Pascha's yacht, the beautiful vessel due to take Pascha back to Puerto Rico later that day, and her ticket home in five days, had toppled over in the storm and beached on its side.

* * *

Pascha held onto his temper by a thread.

Were the fates conspiring against him? How else to explain the run of luck, all of it bad, that had blighted him the past couple of days?

Until Emily had stolen into his office, everything had been running smoothly. Marat had been too taken with the number of zeroes on the buy-out offer to look closely into the provenance of RG Holdings. Not that it would have mattered if he had. So complex was the structure disguising Pascha's involvement, he was certain it would withstand any vigorous scrutiny. And yet…there was always room for doubt. Marat was lazy but there was no telling how deep his lawyers would dig.

There always existed the possibility something could go wrong.

Emily, who had kept her distance while he'd spoken to his staff, joined him and gave a sympathetic grimace. 'Is it salvageable?'

'It's on its side and filling with water as we speak. The chances of getting a crew here within the next few days to attempt a rescue are remote at best.'

'So what happens now?'

He dragged a hand down his face. 'I don't know.'

He moved away from her, crossing over to Luis, who was speaking on his mobile phone. When he got a minute, he would get his charged. For the moment the yacht was taking all his attention. Once he'd got this sorted he would go back, check the dozens of messages that would undoubtedly have piled up and call Zlatan, his lawyer. One thing at a time. Right now it was the loss of his only means of getting off the island that was his priority.

'Any news?' he asked Luis when he disconnected the call he was on.

'The soonest we can get a boat to you is likely to be two days. The other islands took a real battering—the few boats that aren't destroyed are needed to get the injured to the mainland hospital.'

One consolation Pascha could take was that none of his staff here on Aliana had been injured. They'd all escaped with a solitary scratch between them.

He nodded curtly. 'Keep trying,' he said, doing

his best to keep his tone moderate. He could easily pull some strings and get any number of boats to come for him from the mainland. If he were to do that, he could be off the island within a couple of hours. But the real issue was the coral reef. The local islanders knew it well, knew which sections were safe to sail through and which would rip the hull to shreds. Outsiders, the yachtsmen that could come to his rescue, did not. To call them would be to place lives at risk.

For the first time he cursed his refusal to build a landing strip or heliport on the island. He hadn't wanted to destroy the qualities that made Aliana Island so special. It just went to prove that sentimentality got you nowhere.

'Is there anything I can do to help?' Emily asked quietly, appearing at his side.

'Speak to Valeria. At the moment, it's all hands on deck.' He shook his head at the inappropriateness of his comment. The deck of his yacht was submerging by the minute.

It suddenly occurred to him that Emily would want to hear news of her father.

'Let's go to my hut and check my phone for messages.'

However much he would like to blame her—blame anyone—none of this mess was Emily's fault.

There was nothing else he could do here at the jetty. The clean-up was under way. The storm had knocked the power out but the generators were working and would keep them going for at least a fortnight.

They made the short walk to his hut in silence.

He unlocked the door and held it open for her. Her petite figure brushed against his as she passed.

His jaw clenched.

With everything that was going on, the adrenaline pumping through him—the urge to bury himself in her softness, even if just for a short while—was strong.

Instead he sucked in a breath, plugged his charger in and turned his phone on. It lit up immediately, two dozen beeps ringing out in rapid succession.

He listened to his voicemail messages first. Six missed calls: two from his lawyer, one from his PA and three from James. He listened to the latter first.

'Well?' Emily asked, her arms folded so tightly across her chest a sliver of paper would have struggled to get through. Worry was etched all over her face.

'Three messages from James. One asking how to work the dishwasher, one asking if it's okay to cook a pizza in a microwave and one asking where the iron is.'

She relaxed her stance slightly. 'At least we know they're alive.'

'If your brother hasn't killed them both with food poisoning.'

'My dad's not eating anything so he'll be safe.'

He saw straight through her vain attempt at humour. 'He's not eating?'

'All he does is sleep.' She shrugged helplessly. 'Sleep is good. Eventually he comes out of the darkness. Well, normally he does.'

'And James is capable of caring for him?' Now he knew the man microwaved pizza, real doubts had set in.

'Yep. All he has to do is make sure Dad takes

his pills and keep an eye on him throughout the night.'

He could see how badly she was struggling to keep herself together and he admired her efforts. There was so much he admired about her. 'I'm surprised James didn't ask you to pop home and iron for him.'

'He can ask all he likes—I'm happy to cook for my brother but when it comes to ironing he can jolly well do it himself.' She grinned, a forced smile that tugged at his heart. 'I swear, if I ever have a boy I'm going to train him to do every domestic chore going before I let him loose on the world.'

Of course Emily wanted children. A woman as devoted to her family as she was wouldn't think twice about it. It was in her DNA.

A lancing pain settled in his guts. Once, a long time ago, he'd dreamed of having children. A family linked by his blood.

'So you don't completely baby him, then?' he said, forcing his own grin.

The groove in her brow deepened. 'I never baby him. He's just hopelessly undomesticated.'

'I understand that it's normal in a lot of families for the baby to keep the baby role even into adulthood.' That didn't apply to him, though—Marat had gone to great lengths to ensure Pascha never felt like a brother to him, younger or otherwise. Pascha had grown up feeling like an only child with a stranger living in the room next to him. A stranger he had wished with all his heart would accept him.

'James isn't the baby of the family,' she said, sounding offended. '*I* am. He's three years older than me.'

'Really?' He stared at her, looking for a sign that she was teasing him. All he saw was indignation. 'Then why have *you* taken responsibility for your father?'

'James and I share the responsibility.'

'If that's the case, why didn't he move back home to be with your father too? Why was it only you?'

A look he struggled to discern flitted over her face. The closest he could come to describing it was confusion. 'I offered.'

'And James was happy with that? He didn't offer in turn?'

'What is this? Are you trying to turn me against

my brother?' Her brown eyes were wide, the rest of her features tight, and she took a step back.

'Not at all. I'm just trying to understand why you're the one doing everything—*risking* everything: your job, your home—while your brother gets to live his life as normal apart from occasionally acting as a babysitter.'

She looked as if she'd been punched. 'You haven't the faintest idea what you're talking about or what we've been through, so keep your opinions to yourself.'

She left his hut without a goodbye.

Pascha could have kicked himself. He hadn't wanted to upset her, but nonetheless he was glad he'd said what he had.

He would bet every last cent he had that James's job wasn't at risk. The man ran his own business, could take all the leave he needed with no one to answer to.

Emily had been the one to take all the time off, enough to have been given a final warning for it. Emily had been the one to leave her flat and move back into her childhood home.

James might be the elder sibling but it was the

younger of the two who had taken the role of leader.

It was the younger of the two who'd effectively given up her life for their father.

CHAPTER TEN

EMILY SAT AT the table of her hut—which had mercifully escaped the storm with no internal damage—carefully sewing sequins onto the hem of the dress she'd spent the afternoon making, a different dress from the one she'd marked out a couple of days before. So what if she had no mannequin or model? That she was doing something practical was enough.

She remembered the first dress she'd made. She'd been seven. Naturally, her mother had done the majority of the work, but once the work was done she had let Emily raid her button box. Emily had spent hours sewing all the pretty, sparkly ones all over the dress, being very careful not to stab her seven-year-old fingers too often.

She'd loved wearing that dress, had got every ounce of wear from it, leaving a trail of fallen-off buttons wherever she went. More than anything, she'd loved the closeness she'd felt with her mum at that time, a special time only for them.

After her heated exchange with Pascha in his hut, Emily had buried herself in the clean-up, working until long after the sun had gone down, doing everything she was physically capable of. It had been therapeutic. It had left her no time to think.

Today was different.

Today, when she'd shown up at the main lodge at the crack of dawn, Valeria had given her a hug and told her there was nothing else for her to do. All that was left was hard manual work.

Emily had spent the day alone with her thoughts.

She'd thought about a lot of things, especially about what Pascha had said about James; the truth it contained. And, as she'd thought, she'd wandered back to the waterfall and sat on the ledge, gazing at all the bright colours glistening under the sun.

She might loathe the colour pink but she'd always adored bright, happy colours.

When had she stopped designing bright

clothes? When had she stopped wearing them? It was working with Hugo, his love for the gothic and theatrical. His control over his designers was absolute. She'd moulded herself into what she believed he wanted her to be and, worse, had let it spill into her private life. Yes, she adored dressing up, loved wearing make-up, but when had she last worn clothes she felt were for her and not some image she was trying to live up to?

Armed with a determination to fix it, she'd hurried back to her hut, grabbed the roll of Persian Orange cotton, drawn a quick sketch as a guide and got to work.

So what if the finished product was a shambles?

So what if it didn't fit properly?

This was for *her*.

When had she lost the essence of herself?

Had she ever found it in the first place...?

A tap on the door caught her attention and she tilted her head to find Pascha standing there. With all the activity involved in fixing and straightening everything affected by the storm, they'd spent hardly any time together since leaving the shelter.

He'd come to her hut, though, late in the night, so late she'd almost given up hope.

Not that she'd been hoping. She'd been too angry and hurt by his words about James to want him to come to her.

She'd been lying in her bed wide awake when he'd tapped on the same glass door he was currently standing at. That one tap had been enough.

However much she'd wanted to deny it, she'd carried with her a deep, inner yearning, an intense almost cramp-like feeling of helpless excitement.

He'd stood at her door, hands in his pockets. He'd looked shattered.

He'd said two words. 'I'm sorry.'

She'd been in his arms before he'd crossed the threshold.

There had been no more conversation. All their talking had been done through their bodies.

He'd left early.

Now, he stepped into the hut bringing with him a cloud of citrusy manliness.

She closed her eyes, hating the way her heart raced just to see him.

The night was bewitching. Everything felt so

different in the daylight, her emotions so much more exposed.

'Everything okay?' she asked, forcing graciousness as she resumed her sewing.

'I thought you'd want to know—James has called. Your father got out of bed today.'

She turned her head to look at him so quickly she wouldn't have been surprised if she'd given herself whiplash. 'You're joking?'

His eyes were steady. 'No joke.'

While Emily tried to digest this unexpected news, Pascha took the seat opposite her.

She could feel his stare resting on her but suddenly felt too fearful to return it, too scared of what he would read in her eyes. Scared of what she would read in *his* eyes.

Her father had got out of bed. A small step, yes, but one with huge implications. In theory this meant the worst of it was over. She should be celebrating.

So why did she still feel so flat?

'Why didn't you tell me your father tried to kill himself?'

The needle went right into her thumb. 'Ow!' Immediately she stuck her thumb into her mouth.

'Have you hurt yourself?' he asked, his eyes crinkled with concern.

She shook her head before pulling her thumb out of her mouth and examining it. A spot of bright red blood pooled out so she put it back in her mouth and sucked on it.

She was going to kill James.

They'd made a promise to each other. Yes, it had been an unspoken promise, but it was an unspoken promise they'd carried their entire lives. They didn't speak about their father's severe depression outside the family home, not to anyone. It was kept between them. Their father's attempted suicide came under that pact.

So why the hell had James told Pascha Virshilas, of all people?

'Do I take it by the horrified look on your face that you're angry I know?' Pascha asked.

'Yes, I am *very* angry,' she said, her fury so great she could barely get her words out.

'Why? Are you ashamed of him?'

'Of course not! But when my dad's well again I know *he* will be ashamed. He won't want anyone to know.'

'Has he done this before?' Pascha asked quietly.

'What? Tried to kill himself?' Her voice rose.

'I know this is painful for you to talk about but I must know—when did he take the pills?'

'Didn't James tell you that?'

'No. And, before you turn your anger on your brother, he didn't tell me, not directly. It was a throwaway comment about stopping his watch on the medicine cabinet. I don't think he even realised he'd said it.'

Slightly mollified, Emily put the fabric down and made a valiant stab at humour. 'Your powers of deduction astound me.'

To her alarm, Pascha saw right through her attempt to lighten the mood and placed his hand on her wrist. 'I'd already guessed something bad had occurred. This just confirmed it. Now, please answer my question. When did he take the pills?'

Finally she met his gaze head-on. 'When do *you* think he took them?'

He sighed heavily, as if purging his lungs of every fraction of oxygen contained within them.

'He tried to kill himself the same day you suspended him on suspicion of theft. Two months to the day after we'd buried my mother.'

The obvious remorse that seeped out of him as she spoke her words had her feeling suddenly wretched.

She tugged her wrist out of his strong grip but, instead of moving her hand away, rested it atop his. 'He was a man on the edge before you suspended him,' she explained with a helpless shrug. 'What you did pushed him over that edge, and I'm not going to lie to you Pascha: I've spent the past month *hating* you for it.

'But the truth is, my father had just been waiting for an excuse. James and I knew how bad he was becoming. It's like watching a child cross a road with a lorry rushing towards them but not being able to run fast enough to push the child away, or scream loudly enough for them to hear. We couldn't reach him. *I* couldn't reach him. I've never been able to. The only person who could reach him when he fell into that pit was my mother, but she isn't here any more.'

Did Emily realise she had tears pouring down her cheeks? Pascha wondered. Or that her fingers were gripping his hand as if he were the anchor rooting her? His chest hurt to see such naked distress.

'This depression, it's happened before?'

She nodded, running her hand over her face in an attempt to wipe her free-flowing tears away. 'He's always suffered from it but can go months—years—without succumbing. And I know I shouldn't say succumbing, as if it's his fault, because I know it isn't. He can't help it any more than Mum could help getting that monstrous illness.'

Despite her impassioned words, Pascha didn't think she believed them, not fully.

He tried to think how he would have felt if he'd been a child and his father had shut himself away for weeks on end. Children were sensitive and felt things more deeply than most adults credited.

His illness had been devastating for his parents, but they were adults and understood there was nothing they could have done to prevent it. Children were liable to blame themselves.

Just as he was considering which of his contacts would be best placed to recommend a psychiatrist at the top of their field, his phone vibrated, the *Top Cat* tune ringing out loudly.

Emily laughed, tears still brimming in her eyes. 'I love that tune.'

He grinned in response and swiped his phone to answer it.

It was his lawyer, Zlatan.

'I'll call you back,' he said, disconnecting the call. He got to his feet and looked down at her. She'd stopped crying. Her eyes were red and swollen, her cheeks all blotchy. She looked adorable.

'Are you going to be okay? I need to call Zlatan.'

She sniffed and nodded. 'I still can't believe that's your ring tone. *Top Cat* was my favourite cartoon as a child.'

'And mine,' he admitted. 'My father got some black market videos of it from one of his clients. When I was too ill to do anything else, I would watch them over and over.'

Their eyes held and he was taken with the most powerful urge to lean over the table and scoop her into his arms.

Yesterday he'd sworn to himself that whatever was happening between them had to stop.

All he could offer her was money. He knew without having to be told that she didn't want it.

Emily needed someone to love her—someone

who could give her a family all of her own to heap her love on.

And that was the one thing he could never give her.

Despite his best intentions, he'd climbed the stairs leading up to her hut in the dead of night, exhausted after the clean-up and little sleep, and found himself rapping on her door before he'd realised his legs had taken him to her door. Even then, he'd tried to convince himself he was there to apologise, nothing else. Certainly not to make love to her again.

He needed to put some distance between them. Things were becoming too... He didn't know what the word was to describe the growing connection between them, knew only that nothing could ever come of it. 'I need to get going. I have a lot of work to do.'

'I'm going to stay in here and finish this off,' she said, picking up the bright material she'd been working on when he'd walked in. 'And then I might take another walk to the waterfall.'

'It will be dark soon,' he pointed out. 'I would prefer it if you held off until the morning.'

He was rewarded for his concern with a soft

smile. 'If it makes you feel better, I'll wait until the morning.'

'Thank you.'

'And I'll hold off jumping into the pool until I can see the bottom.'

'Very funny.' Not even Emily would be crazy enough to jump into that pool. 'I'll see you later.'

He could feel her eyes following his movements all the way to his own hut.

Emily assumed she would spend the evening in her hut alone as she had the night before. The clean-up was still ongoing, with most of the staff concentrating on clearing the felled trees and other manual jobs.

When Pascha turned up at her hut not long after sundown, he looked more relaxed than she'd ever seen him, the lines around his eyes and mouth softened. Even his clothes were casual, dressed as he was in faded jeans and a white T-shirt. She would never in a million years have guessed he owned a pair of jeans. Or that they would fit so well...

'We're eating on the beach tonight,' he said, not bothering with any preamble.

On the beach…

Had it really only been three days since they'd eaten on the beach, her first night on the island?

It felt a lifetime away. *She* felt a lifetime away.

She'd placed the dress she'd spent the afternoon making on a hanger. It wasn't quite finished; it was missing embellishments she wanted to add to it. But…it was done. A little rough, considering there was no mannequin or model for her to use, but it was done—the only item of real colour in the room.

She was fed up of the dark.

'Give me a minute,' she said, yanking the dress off the hanger and diving into her bathroom. In no time at all, she'd stripped off the black vest and black shorts and donned her creation.

She turned before the mirror, staring critically at her reflection.

Deviating from her original sketch, she'd made it sleeveless, the bodice smocked and elasticated to hold it in place, the skirt flaring out into a 'V' that fell to her knees. She plucked out a couple of loose threads from around the hem then pulled her tortoiseshell comb loose—really, why did she bother with it? Her hair always fell out.

She dashed back into the main room of the hut. 'Two secs,' she said, lunging at the dressing table. Not bothering to sit down, she applied a little eyeliner, some mascara and a dash of coral lipstick.

There was no need for war paint. Pascha had seen her stripped bare, in all senses of the word. And he'd still wanted her. Just as she'd wanted him. Just as she still wanted him, more than she'd ever dreamed possible.

When she turned to face him, the grey of his eyes glittered.

Her thundering heart soared.

'You look…' He raised his shoulders as if to find the word he searched for. 'Like a fire opal.'

Her voice broke. 'Thank you.'

He edged back towards the door. 'We need to go.'

Her skin dancing, she followed him down the steps to the beach.

The staff were already there, setting up long bench tables which were being covered with crockery, cutlery and plentiful bottles of wine and beer. Some of the felled trees and branches had been placed in an A shape to make a bonfire a little further down the beach from where they would be eating.

'I thought everyone could do with a night off to let their hair down,' Pascha murmured into her ear.

Startled, she tilted her face to look at him. His arms were crossed over his broad chest but there was nothing defensive about his stance. It was more a look of a man surveying all he owned and taking immense pride in it.

'What can I do to help?' she asked.

He gave a brief flash of his teeth. 'You can help me with the barbecue.'

'You're cooking?'

'We all muck in but the barbecue is my domain.'

'You've done this before?'

He raised a shoulder. 'A few times.'

He never ceased to surprise her.

It wasn't long before laughter was the predominant sound, laughter and a whole heap of chatter, the two-dozen staff all determined to forget their worries about family and friends on the battered surrounding islands and mainland for one evening. Plates of food and condiments had been brought out and the wine was in full flow. The balmy weather and black sky with stars glittering like tiny jewels only added to the party effect.

The good humour was contagious and spirits were high. Even Pascha, set apart from the rest of them at the barbecue, had a smile on his face. Emily went backwards and forwards from the industrial-sized barbecue to the tables, delivering trays of ribs, chicken breasts, king prawns, skewer kebabs... The list of food was endless.

So busy did she make herself, and so many conversations did she strike up, that she spent hardly any time with Pascha. That didn't stop her awareness of him.

For a man desperate to get off the island, he was clearly in his element. No one looking at him would think he wished to be elsewhere.

Noticing his glass of beer was empty, she poured another for him and took it over. 'Are you coming to sit down?'

'I'll get these chops finished and then I'll be over,' he promised, taking the glass from her. 'Thanks for this.'

'You're welcome.' His smile made her belly

flip over and her heart soar. She hurried back to the benches with a skip in her walk.

Pascha watched as Emily sat down with his maintenance guys, an animated conversation breaking out.

He wished he could build a rapport with people as easily as she did but he was not one for making friends. He'd missed so much of his schooling due to illness that by the time he'd been well enough to return he'd become an outsider. Five years was a long time in a small child's life. He'd been an outsider ever since, never knowing or learning how to fit in. If it hadn't been for Andrei taking him under his wing, giving him confidence enough not to care when peers had parties to which he was never invited, who knew where he would be today? He'd found his own niche to fit into because he'd always been aware there was nowhere else he *could* fit. Even being tucked under Andrei's wing had come at the price of Marat's hatred for him increasing exponentially.

Was that why he'd been so desperate to hold on to Yana—because he'd felt he'd found a niche with her and had wanted to hold onto it at any cost?

He tried to imagine what his life would have been like if he hadn't, finally, recognised that the cloudy diamond she'd turned into had been a mask for her misery. What kind of a couple would they have been if he hadn't set her free?

The icy clenching in his guts told him the answer to that.

He looked back at Emily. Had he even stopped looking at her?

That dress she'd made…

His fire opal had come to life, dazzling him with her vibrancy. If she were to tread the same path as Yana, and be emotionally blackmailed into forgoing her most basic desires, would her lustre fade too?

He would never know. He would never allow her to set off on that path.

He took a seat at the end of the table and looked at her anew, watching her be dragged to her feet to dance around the bonfire with a bunch of his younger staff. The skirt of her gorgeous dress swirled as she moved to the music being played by his gardener, Oliver, who was singing reggae songs as he strummed on his guitar. Her delicate arms clapped and swayed, her black curls fanning in all directions. He could feel the warmth radiating from her.

It drew him to her.

An ache formed in his chest and he swigged at his beer, as if the act of swallowing could loosen it. It didn't.

From the distance of the bonfire where the embers lit her up, making her beautiful face seem almost ethereal, she caught his gaze. She stilled for a moment before one of the girls grabbed her hand and pulled her into a dance that involved lots of hip-shaking.

He could watch her for hours.

His heart seemed to stutter when she scooped up little Ava, Valeria's two-year-old niece who lived on the island with her parents, who also worked for him.

He couldn't hear Ava's squeals of delight but he could feel them. They hit him deep in his guts.

Emily would be a fantastic mother, fierce and loving, just as his mother had been to him before he'd thrown all her love back in her face.

He could still see the ashen hue of her skin when he'd walked out that final time.

'Pascha,' she'd said. 'Andrei loves you. He would never put Marat above you, only equal to you.'

'You weren't there,' he'd sneered, his anger and hurt turning outward. 'He thinks Marat is deserving of a place on the board by virtue of his *Plushenko blood*.'

'He didn't mean it like that…'

He hadn't let her finish. 'So now you're taking his side? I thought I could expect support from my own mother.'

'It isn't a case of taking sides…'

'From where I'm standing it is. And I can see you have made your choice. I might have wished for your support but I certainly do not need it. I'm finished with this excuse for a family and its obsession with bloodlines. This cuckoo is leaving the nest.'

He could still see the confusion in her eyes at his parting comment.

Would he have reacted differently if he hadn't received the test results mere days before, if his dream of having his own blood family hadn't been crushed?

He didn't know. All he remembered feeling was hopelessness as he realised that his life meant nothing. That *he* meant nothing. The woman who had borne him, the one person in the world he shared a bloodline with, had failed to take his side. He was alone. Isolated. So he'd forced Yana to stay, desperate to hold onto something to validate his life.

It had taken almost two years of misery, as he threw himself into work, determined to make a success of himself on his own, before he'd seen what he was doing to her and set her free.

Luis joined him, forcing him to switch his attention away from memories that speared his heart and onto easy talk of boats and island life. By the time Luis had slapped his back and wished him goodnight, Emily was no longer dancing.

Automatically he looked out to the lagoon, his lips curving into a smile to see her paddling out to calf height.

He got to his feet.

At the water's edge, he removed his footwear and rolled his jeans up.

'I knew that was you,' Emily said, turning her head to smile at him. There hadn't been an atom of doubt in her mind that the person wading into the lagoon behind her was Pascha.

'I'm just making sure you're not planning on going for a swim.'

'I was thinking about it,' she admitted. 'Maybe later when everyone's gone to bed. You should join me.'

She'd come out for a paddle because she'd needed space. She'd needed to put a little distance between her and Pascha before she ran over and dragged him onto the makeshift sandy dance floor.

She'd felt his eyes on her as she danced. Whenever she could no longer resist, she'd peeked back, her heart tugging to see him alone nursing his beer, setting himself apart while the party he'd instigated went on around him.

'Wading to my calves is enough for me,' he said. 'Not all the marine life in the lagoon is friendly, especially at night.'

'Is that your way of telling me not to go for a midnight swim?'

'It's my way of asking you to consider the dangers of doing it.'

She laughed softly. 'I've probably had too much to drink to swim.' Not that she was drunk. A little merry, maybe, but probably more than was safe to go swimming alone.

Pascha standing beside her made her feel giddy in a completely different way; her blood fizzed at his closeness.

'I'm glad to hear it,' he said, his voice dry.

'I'll save my swimming for the waterfall tomorrow,' she couldn't resist saying before laughing. 'Do you have any idea how lucky you are, owning this island? You've got your own lagoon and your own waterfall!'

'I do know how lucky I am.'

Something in his tone made her stare at him, made her realise that up to that point she'd avoided his gaze.

With the darkness of the sky enveloping them it was impossible to read his eyes; she knew only that something glittered there that made her heart double over.

In the distance, Oliver was singing a Bob Marley classic, the remaining partygoers singing along, the music blurring with the gentle lapping of the waves around them.

Pascha's chest rose and he looked up to the stars before staring back down at her. He reached out a hand and caught a ringlet.

All the breath rushed out of her body as he leaned his head forward.

She had no idea what profound comment he would say next, and certainly didn't expect the mirth that spread over his face. 'You smell like a bonfire.'

His fingers still played with her curl. He'd moved closer to her, near enough for her to feel the heat of his body.

The amusement left his face. He dropped her curl and dragged his fingers down the mane of her hair to her shoulders, then brushed up her neck to gently cup her throat.

His breath was hot on her skin. She closed her eyes. Her lips tingled, anticipating his kiss…

'You could make a man lose himself, Emily Richardson,' he murmured into her ear, before releasing his hold.

She snapped her eyes back open to find him striding through the water back to shore.

She spent the night in her cabin alone.

CHAPTER ELEVEN

EMILY SAT ON the ledge watching the sun make its ascent, the moonlit silver slowly vanishing, shades of blues and greens emerging. The only sound was the steady rush of the waterfall opposite. It glistened in a multitude of colours.

At best she'd managed a few hours of sleep. Every time she'd closed her eyes all she'd been able to see was Pascha's face. He'd been there when she'd opened them too. He was everywhere.

She'd been so sure he was going to kiss her. When he'd walked away she'd felt such rejection despite the strange words he'd uttered. Those feelings were still there but also in the mix was the euphoria of a whole evening with no worries. The impromptu party had been exactly what she had needed. Pascha had made it happen. It hadn't been for her, it had been for his staff, but it was all down to him. All the anxiety that had held her in a noose for the best part of a year had slipped away.

But now, here at the waterfall, her head felt crammed.

Her father was going to be all right. She could feel it. Such a small thing, getting out of bed. Given the state he'd been in, though, it was a huge thing. It showed willingness.

The road ahead wouldn't be easy but for the first time she allowed herself to believe the road ahead would have him travelling on it.

The relief was indescribable.

But mingled with the relief was something else. It shamed her. As childish and selfish as she knew it to be, she couldn't help feeling despondent that it was for James that he'd made that first step. Not for her. It didn't matter what she did or how hard she tried, it was never for her.

It shouldn't matter. It *really* shouldn't matter. That he was treading the first steps on the path to recovery was enough. She'd done everything she could to help him, given up so much. Surely now…

Surely now it was time for her to start living again?

And she knew just the way to start.

She got to her feet and peered over the edge. A thrill of anticipation rushed through her. She unwrapped her sarong and placed it on the grass, then slipped her flip-flops off.

Another image of Pascha came into her mind. If he knew what she was about to do, he would probably tie her to a chair for the rest of her stay. It was one of the reasons she'd started the trail before the sun had come up.

She forced his image away.

Adrenaline pumping, she took a few paces backwards and then ran, jumping high into the air right at the very last second.

Those few moments of weightlessness were indescribable, exhilarating: the heady rush of flying combining with the hint of danger at what lay beneath the clear water.

Keeping the presence of mind to point her toes and hold onto her neck, she entered the cool water at incredible speed. Down she went, lower and lower into the pool, waiting to hit the bottom.

* * *

The sun had not long risen when Pascha awoke with a start.

He'd slept well enough but his dreams had been fitful. He'd woken to the vivid image of Emily jumping off the ledge and into the waterfall.

He threw on a pair of shorts and raced to her hut.

It came as no surprise to find it empty.

His subconscious had been telling him something.

He made it to the waterfall in a third of the usual time, his body drenched in sweat.

Her possessions were at the base of the ledge. Blood pounding in his head, he peered cautiously over it.

He caught a flash of ebony hair.

Squinting to get a better focus, he saw her properly, legs stretched out, arms resting back atop a crop of rocks at the edge of the waterfall, the stream of water pouring over her steadier than the torrent flowing in the centre.

She must have sensed him for her head lifted and she raised an arm in a wave. She called out but her voice was muffled by the waterfall.

It was not until she beckoned him that he re-alised she was asking him to join her.

He cupped his hands around his mouth and yelled, 'Don't be ridiculous.'

Shaking her head, she got to her feet and dived into the pool, staying submerged for so long the breath caught in his throat.

When she resurfaced she swam to the other end of the pool and hauled herself out. 'Jump in,' she called up to him, now far enough away from the waterfall for her voice to carry.

'No!'

'I promise you, it's the most exhilarating feel-ing in the world.'

She was too far away for him to see her fea-tures clearly but there was a definite air of ela-tion about her.

Pascha did not take risks. Having come so close to death at such a young age, when the question of whether he lived or died had been completely out of his control, he had determined always to decide his own fate. He did not com-promise his safety and he *never* put it solely in the hands of others.

Less than ten hours earlier he'd been tempted

to throw off his clothes and swim into the lagoon in the dark. *She'd* made him want to do that with the sparkle in her eyes as she'd looked out over the lagoon, the sense of an adventure waiting to happen.

The temptation he'd felt had been real. But not half as real or as consuming as the temptation to pull her into his arms and taste those delectable lips all over again. He'd wanted to taste all of her all over again. He still did.

If it had been just the two of them at the beach, he doubted he would have had the presence of mind to hold himself back. His staff surrounding him had kept his control—his sanity—in check. He'd lain in his large, lonely bed and fought the greater temptation to take himself to her, as he'd done the night before, and slip beneath her covers; to make love to her all over again. Because that was exactly what it felt like: making love. And that was the greatest danger of all.

And now she wanted him to jump forty feet with only her word that it was safe.

'Pascha, trust me. Keep your feet together and hold onto your neck. You will love it, I promise. Trust me.'

Trust her? Put his control and safety in the hands of another?

Despite all his self-imposed safety mechanisms, his body zinged, as if it were trying to take possession of his mind.

Her madness must bc contagious.

Focusing solely on the raven-haired beauty perched like a mermaid on the pool's edge, he removed his boots.

All you have to do is run and jump.

He hadn't run on anything other than a treadmill since he'd been fourteen.

His legs had had enough of his procrastination.

Almost as if it were happening to someone else and he was watching from afar, he took the short run and jumped.

Those few seconds of flying felt like nothing else in the world.

As gravity sucked his body down to the clear blue abyss, all Pascha could think was that she was right: this was the most exhilarating feeling in the world.

He hit the water, landing with an enormous splash. It consumed him, as if he were being dragged to the centre of the earth.

He refused to panic, keeping a clear head through the enormous shot of adrenaline the jump had produced. Pointing his arms upwards, he propelled his body up until he broke the surface.

The first thing he saw was the relief on Emily's face, a look that was immediately replaced with the brightest, most beautiful smile he had ever seen.

'You did it!' She laughed, a sweet, lyrical sound that warmed his heart. 'You really did it.'

He swam over, caught hold of her thighs and pulled her down into the water, using his arms to trap her against the edge of the rocks. He tried to catch his breath, tried to suck oxygen into his burning lungs, but all he could focus on was the beam of her smile.

The swell of her breasts pushed against his chest but she made no move to escape the confinement. Instead, she rested her hands on his shoulders and gazed at him, her chest hitching, an intensity swirling in her eyes that drove into his veins and paralysed him.

Her thighs brushed against his. A charge

careered through him, so powerful he could feel it singe his blood.

He wanted to lose himself again in the wonders of her—the woman who made his senses come alive. The only woman capable of making him forget himself.

Her eyes had transformed into liquid. Her lips parted.

And then there was no more staring.

There was no slow build and no tentative caresses either. They simply fused into one, plundering each other's mouths with scorching fierceness.

Her fingers dug possessively into his scalp, her legs lifting and wrapping around his waist, whether by his instigation or her own volition he could not say.

She moaned into his mouth and wrapped her thighs ever tighter, the movement making him realise he'd lost his shorts during the jump. The only barrier between his rampaging erection and her welcoming warmth was the flimsy material of her bikini bottoms.

For the first time in nearly two decades he had to grit his teeth to stop himself losing all control.

He needed air. He needed to feel the ground beneath his feet before he lost all contact with reality.

In one motion he lifted her out of the water, pulled himself out and tumbled down onto the grassy bank, pinning her beneath him.

The expression in her eyes… Never had he seen such openness reflected back at him. No inhibitions, nothing except honest, naked desire.

Her hand snaked around his head to cradle his skull and pull him down for another kiss. Devouring the sweetness of her mouth, he roved a hand down her side, exploring the soft, creamy skin. Her bikini top was secured by a tie around her back. It took no effort to untie it and whip the top away.

The feel of her naked breasts crushed beneath his chest fired him anew and he dipped his head down to capture a dusky nipple in his mouth.

She responded to his caresses with more passion than he could ever have dreamed.

He needed to kiss her again and, as he lost himself in the headiness of it all, Emily twisted from beneath him and climbed on top, straddling him.

For what felt an age in which his heart beat a thousand times she did nothing but stare at him, her eyes scanning every inch of his face.

She traced a thumb over his lips, a feather of a movement that was both tender and erotic, before replacing her thumb with her mouth.

His hands reached round and held her tightly against him as she ground against his erection.

She gave a low moan followed by the breath of a sigh, then nibbled at his neck, teasing, painless.

Covering his face and neck with kisses, tasting the muskiness of his skin, Emily slipped a hand between their meshed bodies, running her fingers down his lightly haired chest all the way to his mass of dark, wiry hair.

A deep pulsation seeped through her when she encircled his erection. She closed her eyes and thrilled at its heavy weight, the silken feel of its length.

Never, never had she imagined she could feel like this, feel such a need to be possessed. And it was all him: Pascha. He *did* something to her, ignited feelings—sensuous and emotional—she had never known existed within her. And those feelings were growing.

When she opened her eyes, she found his gaze locked upon her, his magnetic eyes stark with his desire. For her.

Whatever his reasons for keeping his distance last night, at that moment it didn't matter. All that did matter was this moment, and this moment was with Pascha, the man who made her body come alive and her heart sing.

He cupped her cheeks and half-rose to meet her mouth, devouring it with his hot tongue, their kisses becoming increasingly desperate.

His fingers played with the ties holding the sides of her bikini bottoms together. She raised her hips a touch, her gasps deepening when he untied them and pulled the scraps of material off, discarding them on the grass beneath them.

Now they were both naked, the burn inside her turning to lava.

His mouth closed back over hers, large hands running over her back, tracing the arch of her shoulder blades and up, digging into her scalp, dragging through her hair. And all the while the tension within her grew. She'd never known desire could be a living thing.

And then she remembered where they were.

And remembered that Pascha had lost his shorts in the pool. Even if he carried condoms with him they would be gone.

It took every ounce of her control to break away from his kisses and the heavenly things he was doing to her, grab his wrist and pin him to the grass.

Still straddling him, she gazed down at the face she could never grow tired of staring at. 'I'm not on the pill.'

The intensity in his eyes concentrated, a pulse firing from them that made her belly somersault.

'Emily, I can't...' He swallowed. 'All my treatment as a child left me sterile. I promise I am clean and I promise you'll be safe.'

Her heart twisted. She returned the strength of his stare, trying to reach through and read his mind. Read his heart.

He was sterile...?

He was asking for her trust...?

She *did* trust him.

She might have been forced to the island but he was doing everything in his power to keep her safe while she was there.

Pascha did not take risks. Making unprotected

love definitely constituted risky by anyone's standards, but doubly so for him.

Her heart twisted again as she realised that this promise meant that he must trust her too.

He'd trusted her enough to make the jump…

He'd trusted her enough to share his secret— one which, instinct told her, haunted him.

Unable to stop herself, she released his wrists and planted her lips on his, a hard yet tender kiss that he responded to with a growl, his arms snaking around her waist.

The tip of his erection pressed against her opening, almost teasing her. She raised her groin a little higher, consumed with the need to *be* consumed.

The strong thud of his heart hammering against his chest reverberated through her skin, matching the unsteady tempo of her own.

Slowly she sank onto him, finding his lips, his breath flowing into her pores and filling her mouth with his heat just as he was filling her.

Skin on skin.

There were no words.

Nothing could ever describe the total bliss filling her.

With Pascha's hand steadying her, she started to move. Gripping the sides of his head, her sensitised breasts brushing against his chest, she ground against him, a steady, almost lazy tempo, the pulsations within her deepening.

A glazed look came into his eyes but the total connection between them remained, fusing them so deeply that she lost any sense of where he began and she ended.

Pure, pure pleasure.

Her orgasm started out as a low surge rippling through her, setting alight every atom of her being. Higher and higher it climbed until it peaked in an explosion of colour.

A strangled groan escaped his lips and he bucked into her, holding her tight against him, prolonging the moment for them both.

She rode the crest for as long as she could before floating back to earth, the softest landing.

Emily expelled a contented sigh.

Her face was buried in his neck, his strong hands stroking her back, holding her tight to him, Pascha twisted onto his side so he could look down at her.

A lock of ebony hair lay damp across her forehead. He smoothed it away, pressing a kiss to the newly exposed skin.

'Why are you staring at me like that?' she asked, tracing a lazy finger up and down his forearm.

'Because I like staring at you. You're beautiful.'

'I think *you're* beautiful.'

'A very macho description,' he said with a laugh, and rolled onto his back, pulling her with him

The sun's rays were increasing, bathing them in a warm pool of light. Pascha could almost imagine it was just the two of them on the planet. If it were just the two of them left on Earth, Pascha reflected, he doubted he would ever be bored. Emily kept him on his toes.

'What possessed you to make the jump?' he asked after long, serene minutes had passed. 'Anything could have happened to you.'

'But it didn't.'

'But it could have.'

She raised her head and smiled. 'Pascha, this waterfall has clearly been evolving for hundreds of thousands of years, and the pool with it. I knew it would be deep.'

'But you couldn't have known what was beneath the waterline. There could have been rocks or anything. You could have killed yourself.' A coldness crept into his bones at the thought.

'But I didn't.'

'But what if you had? Where would that leave your father? Your brother?' *Me*, he almost added, the thought coming from nowhere.

'I don't know.' She bit into her lip and stared at him. 'They have each other. It was on James's watch that my dad got out of bed.'

'You've been there the rest of the time.' From what Pascha understood, Emily had been there the whole time. She'd given up the independence of her home and put her job in jeopardy for her father.

'From what's happened since I left, it's obvious that the only person my dad needed was James. Not me.' She broke the stare and tugged herself out of his arms, sitting up. 'I've tried so hard. All my life I've tried.'

'Tried for what?'

She turned her face back to him and raised her shoulders. 'To be enough.'

'Enough for what?'

'For him to hold on to.' She shook her head. 'In all honesty, Mum was the only one he really responded to when he was ill, but James would tell him a joke and sometimes Dad would smile. I'd tell him a joke—normally the same one as James—and he never responded. Never. When he was well, he was wonderful with me, but when he was ill it was as if I didn't exist. I was never enough. I guess I'm still not.'

'I don't believe that,' he said carefully, rubbing a hand over her naked back. She had the softest skin. 'Your father loves you.'

'I know he loves me.' Her voice was sad. 'It's just not enough, is it? Not if I can't help him.'

He placed a kiss to the small of her back. 'You've done more for your father than anyone could have wished. It is time for you to forget about your relationship with him as a child. Focus on the future.' He kissed her again, a little higher. 'I would sell my soul if I could have a future with my father.'

'I know. You're right.'

'Of course I'm right.'

'Your arrogance never gets old.'

He swiped at her nose before wrapping his legs around her and pulling her so she leant back against him.

'Can I ask you something?'

'You're asking my permission?' He was certain she was going to ask about his sterility. As if there was anything to be discussed. It was a fact of life—a fact of *his* life—something he'd long ago accepted. Just as he'd accepted it prevented him from having the future he'd always craved.

'It was something you said before about you and your father building Plushenko's between you. I always thought it was a really old firm, like Fabergé.'

'That was clever marketing—we wanted people to believe that.' He breathed in a sigh of relief as he realised it wasn't the subject he'd thought she was going to broach. At that moment, wrapped around Emily, he was as close to peace as he'd ever been.

He couldn't regret making love to her again. He would never regret it. For now, all he wanted was to hold onto it for a little longer.

As he inhaled, he captured the scent of her hair. Even with her swim in the pool and the spray of the waterfall he could still catch the faint scent of the light, fruity shampoo she favoured.

'In a way, you can thank my leukaemia for the founding of Plushenko's,' he said. 'I had to undergo five years of chemotherapy and steroids and a host of other medicines. To keep me alive cost money. The only way to afford it was for Andrei—the man I called Papa—to work all the hours he could. At the time he was earning minimal wages as a jewellery maker for a middle-of-the-road Russian jeweller. He started to produce his own bespoke pieces, working every spare hour in the workshop he built at the back of our house. Those pieces paid for my medications and, unwittingly, formed the basis of the company known today as Plushenko's.'

'He sounds like an amazing man.'

'He was,' Pascha agreed.

'Do you think all the attention Andrei paid you, and all the hours he spent working to earn money for your treatment, made Marat jealous?' she asked.

He breathed her in deeply. 'I don't remember Marat ever liking me.' Knowing how much Marat loathed his very existence had done nothing to stop Pascha's idolisation of him. For years he'd wanted nothing more than Marat's acceptance. A part of him still longed for it.

'Have you thought of trying again with him?' she said. 'I know you said you offered to buy Plushenko's a number of years ago, but you were probably both feeling raw; it was so soon after your father had died. Maybe time has mellowed him.'

'I can't take the risk.'

'Why not?'

Because if it blows up in my face I will lose the chance to save Andrei's legacy. And if I lose that I will never be able to convince my mother how sorry I am.'

'Are you still estranged from her too?'

He nodded. 'I sought her out after Andrei's funeral. I apologised for our estrangement. I told her about the island I'd bought in her name but she didn't want to know.' She'd rejected him, just like Pascha had rejected her.

'Words aren't always enough,' she said softly. 'It's our actions that prove our love.'

'Is that why you went out of your way, at your own risk and with a real possibility of arrest, to help your father?' he said with more acid than he would have liked. 'Is that why you've given up your home and sacrificed your job, so he has living proof of how much you love him?'

She froze in his arms. When she next spoke, her words were measured but had a definite catch to them. 'The one thing I know with any certainty is that our time on this earth is limited. And you know it too.'

She didn't say anything else. She didn't need to.

They'd both lost people who'd meant the world to them.

But Emily's situation was different and not just because she'd been secure in her mother's love. Emily had never wounded someone she loved so badly that forgiveness was only an elusive dream. And, if she ever did wound someone she loved to that extent, she would be forgiven without having to prove her worth. Whatever darkness resided in her father's head, he did love her. She wasn't inherently unlovable. She didn't have something missing like he did. The blood that ran through the Richardson clan's veins tied them together, made them a part of each other.

He shared his mother's blood but still she couldn't forgive him.

With a start he realised it had been almost three years since he'd asked her forgiveness at Andrei's funeral.

Emily had lost her mother three months ago and the pain was still very much there on the surface.

He'd lived through a dark fog for at least a year after Andrei had died.

His mother and Andrei had been soul mates. Was it any wonder she'd lashed out at him when he'd said, five years too late, that he was sorry?

'I'm sorry,' he whispered, brushing her hair with the flat of his hand. 'I know your need to help your father comes from the love you have for him.' She had more love in her heart than anyone he'd ever met before.

Emily rubbed his arm in silent understanding then leaned forward slightly to swipe a small bug off her thigh. As she did so, his attention was captured by a tiny blue blur on the base of her spine. 'Sit forward.'

She shifted a little and he was able to see it clearly: another butterfly tattoo, smaller yet more intricate than the one on her ankle.

'I got it done just after my mum died,' she explained, craning her neck to look at him. 'We had our ankle ones done together.'

'Your mum had a tattoo?'

She nodded with a whimsical smile. 'She'd always wanted one. When we got the diagnosis that her illness was terminal, we went to a tattoo parlour and had identical ones done. I wanted this one as my own private memory of her.'

Pascha stared at the private memorial a beat longer, feeling like he had just had his own butterfly let loose in his chest.

He gently pushed her forward some more so he could kiss the butterfly. She truly tasted like the honey scent she carried.

A gasp escaped her throat as he trailed his tongue up her spine, all the way to the base of her neck.

'Enough talk.' He knelt behind her and cupped a breast, savouring its creamy weight. He felt as if he could savour it—savour her—for ever.

CHAPTER TWELVE

HE MUST HAVE dozed off. Totally spent, Pascha had gathered Emily into his arms and lain back down on the grass with a heart hammering loudly enough to frighten any wildlife.

He'd held her close, inhaling the musty scent of their sex, and a solid form of contentment had stolen over him.

For the first time in his life, he'd truly let go of himself. Emily did that to him. Somehow she was able to tap into parts of him he'd hidden for so long he'd forgotten they'd ever been there.

As a child he'd dreamt of driving fast cars. Now, as an adult, he owned more fast cars than his childhood self had known existed—but he drove them cautiously, all too aware of what other drivers on the road could do.

His childhood self would have been disgusted that he'd never taken one of his fast cars onto a track and put his foot down just for the sheer hell of the ride.

He had no way of knowing the time but, judging by the position of the sun almost directly over them, it must have been getting on for midday.

Emily looked so sweet curled on him with her hair spread across his chest that he felt cruel waking her. But he had no choice. He should have headed back to the lodge hours ago. Before he'd made love to her. Before he'd been foolish enough to go against everything he believed in and jumped off the ledge.

Both were equally dangerous in their own way.

He had a sudden image of his small childhood self, fist-pumping at seeing him fly off the ledge and into the pool. Yes, younger, childhood Pascha would have approved of *that*. But that was before he had learned how precarious life could be.

'We need to go back,' he said, kissing her shoulder before giving it a gentle shake.

She opened her eyes and smothered a yawn. 'Already?'

'I should have word if someone is available to get me to the mainland.' For all he knew, someone knowledgeable about the coral reef might have already made the trip to Aliana Island and, unable to locate him, returned to their own island. Try as he might, he couldn't bring himself to care. He wanted to hold onto this moment while he was living it. Before he had to say goodbye to her.

Emily got to her feet and tied her bikini bottoms back together.

'Where's my top?' He didn't have a chance to look for it before she spotted it and walked a couple of feet to retrieve it. Keeping her back to him, she put it on, tying it together at the back in a bow. Done, she turned back to him. 'So, Sherlock, how do we get out of here?'

'You mean to say you jumped into the pool without an escape route planned?' He didn't know whether to laugh or shout.

'You jumped too,' she pointed out with a grin.

'I assumed you'd already thought of a way out before *you* jumped.' He'd thought no such thing. At the time he hadn't been thinking of anything but her. If he'd been thinking a fraction more coherently, he would never have made the jump.

As they scanned their surroundings, he caught

sight of his shorts floating at the edge of the pool. He fished them out and wrung as much water as he could out of them. He was stepping into them when Emily pointed to the right of the waterfall.

'Look,' she said, 'that incline there seems to have some natural gradients—we should be able to climb up it.'

'It's the most plausible way out,' he agreed, not seeing any other way.

He'd barely finished speaking before Emily darted over to it. She didn't even pause when she reached it.

Open-mouthed, his heart seeming to stop, he watched with a combination of horror and admiration as she began to scale the incline, her bare feet white against the rock.

Where did she get this fearlessness from?

And did he follow in her wake or wait at the base to catch her if she should fall…? Not that she showed any sign of falling; her movements were focused and assured.

From his vantage point he had an excellent view of her bottom and couldn't help the half-smile that twitched on his lips.

'Come on, slow-coach,' she called down to

him, pausing for a moment. 'After a couple of feet it's more scrambling than climbing. Honestly, it's fine.'

She'd said similar words right before he'd jumped. Despite himself, and all the protection he placed around himself, he'd believed her. He'd trusted her. He still did.

He trusted her completely.

Taking a deep, steadying breath, he placed a hand on a ridge and carefully began to climb.

He refused to look down until he made it to the top, which came a lot more quickly than he'd expected.

'Do you have no fear?' he asked, catching his breath. Who needed to work out in a gym? A morning with Emily Richardson provided enough exercise and adrenaline to last a month.

'Of course I do. I just don't feel the need to do a full risk assessment first.' Emily flashed him a half-grin. 'Don't get me wrong, I'm not a die-hard thrill-seeker or anything, but when the opportunity comes to experience something new or different I want to take it.'

It was just another part of herself that she'd suppressed in recent times. Well, no more.

She wrapped her sarong around her waist and slipped her feet into her flip-flops, all the while wishing they didn't have to leave this spot. Not yet.

But the time was inching closer.

In a few short hours Pascha would be leaving the island. Leaving her.

The thought made her throat close and her heart constrict.

She didn't want him to go. Not without her.

His pace was slower than the long strides he usually took. With his hand clasping hers firmly, hope began to stir.

She hadn't been with a man for more years than she could count. It was for a whole host of reasons that she'd avoided relationships and one of them—probably the most minor reason of the lot—was because she'd been waiting to find a man who made her heart beat faster just to think of him; a man who made her go figuratively weak at the knees.

Pascha did all that. He made her feel more than she'd ever felt in her life.

He wasn't the monster she'd thought him at the beginning. He was just a man, a mortal with his own demons to conquer, trying hard to make amends for a past it hurt her heart to think about.

In his office, she'd imagined sex with him would be perfunctory and proper. How she wished she'd been right. Maybe then the need within her would have been extinguished with disappointment, not quadrupled and morphed into something so huge her brain struggled to comprehend it.

But, what her brain struggled to recognise, her heart knew.

Her heart knew she was falling in love with him…

'When we get back to the lodge we'll learn if there's a boat available to take us back to Puerto Rico,' Pascha said, breaking through her dumbfounded thoughts. 'If there is, you will need to pack.'

'I'm coming with you?' That little bit of hope stirred a little stronger.

He gave a rueful smile. 'I have no good reason to keep you here, not any more. I know you won't say anything about the Plushenko deal.'

Stunned at this unexpected development, Emily stopped walking. 'Thank you.'

'I will speak to Zlatan, my lawyer, as soon as we return to the lodge and get the money transferred into your father's bank account. I will also have an official letter drawn up exonerating him of any wrong-doing and leaving the door open for him to return to his job if and when he feels able to.'

'Have you had the case investigated?' she asked hopefully.

'I do not believe your father took that money deliberately. We still need to trace exactly where it went and make moves to retrieve it but that's nothing for you to worry about.'

'That's—'

She tried to speak but he cut her off by cupping her cheeks with his strong hands. 'I want you to know how sorry I am that I didn't get this situation resolved when it first occurred. I like matters of theft, which is what I believed it to be, to be investigated by my personal legal team. Because I had them working flat-out on the Plushenko buyout, your father's case was put to one side. I can't express how deep my regret is for what your father's been through. I am very much aware that I have contributed to his mental decline. Please let him know that if he chooses not to return as my employee I will give him an excellent reference.'

Emily was at a loss for what to say. Pascha's words were like music to her ears. In the end, all she could do was rise onto her toes and place a gentle kiss on his lips. 'Thank you.'

'Don't thank me. It should never have come to this in the first place.'

'You've had a lot on your plate.'

'And don't make excuses for me.' She caught the fleeting ghost of a smile on his handsome features before he released his hold on her and stepped back, running a hand through his hair. 'Come; let's get you back to the lodge and see if we can get you home. I know how badly you want to return to your family.'

Did she? Did she really? She was certainly anxious to see for herself that her father had made an improvement, but did she really want to go back to that same life, a life where she lived for everyone else rather than herself?

She'd been like that in all her relationships.

With a jolt she realised that Pascha was the first person ever to have really known her, stripped back. When they'd first met she'd been too anxious and angry to put on any kind of face for him.

He'd seen *her*, the rawness, all the components that made her Emily, and he hadn't rejected her.

No wonder her few relationships had failed. She'd moulded herself into what she'd thought her boyfriends wanted her to be. And they'd seen through it, become bored with a woman who agreed with everything they said and was always obliging, doing what they wanted.

She'd been right: she hadn't been enough for any of them. How could she have been when she'd never been enough for herself?

Pascha had only ever seen her as herself and still he'd wanted her.

The question now was whether he would still want her when they were away from this spot of paradise.

Emily stood at the back of the yacht watching Aliana Island shrink away, blinking back hot tears. This could be the last time she saw it.

In less than a week her world had changed irrevocably.

The island had become little more than a speck on the horizon when Pascha joined her on the deck.

When they'd got back to the lodge, his hair had been mussed, his jaw covered with dark stubble. He'd looked wild and devilishly sexy.

Since their return he'd showered and shaved, styled his hair and dressed into a beautifully ironed open-necked white shirt and dark-grey trousers. Even his black belt looked as if it had been pressed. Add a tie and blazer, and he could step into any boardroom.

His wildness had gone but he still looked devilishly sexy.

'Am I going to see you again?' she asked, staring up at him and taking the bull by the horns. One thing she had learned during the past few days was that she needed to control her own destiny. If there were changes to be made then she had to be the one to make them.

She saw rather than heard him draw in a breath, his mouth compressing, his features contorting into something that looked like pain. That same pain shot straight into her heart.

'Do I take that as a no?'

Pascha watched as a whole swathe of emotions flittered over Emily's face. The one that struck the strongest chord with him was the fleeting anguish she hadn't been quick enough to conceal. It hurt him to see it.

He should never have given in to his desire, should have fought it harder. And now he had to hurt a woman who had already been through too much pain. But the alternative would only cause her far more.

'Emily, I'm sorry; you and I can never be together.' He needed to spell it out to her. He didn't want there to be any misunderstandings. She deserved the truth.

That familiar groove appeared.

'I need you to understand. It isn't you. It's me.'

Now her features darkened, her lips thinning, her shoulders hunching together.

'I know that's a line a lot of men use, but in this case it's the truth.' He reached out to capture a lock of ebony hair. She flinched away from him, stepping back. 'Emily, we can return to Europe and pick up where we leave off here—enjoy each other's company and have fantastic sex—but nothing can ever come of it. We have no future. *I* can't give you a future.'

'How do you know that?' she whispered.

'Because I can't give you the babies you want.'

She wrapped her arms around herself. 'I don't recall us ever discussing children.'

'We didn't need to. I *know* you and I know family is everything to you.' He remembered the light in her face when she'd been swinging little Ava in the air. If there was a woman made to be a mother, this woman was it. 'I know you want children, and one day you will have them, but I can't be the man to give them to you. I almost destroyed my ex-fiancée over it and I won't destroy you too.'

Emily loosened her arms, a questioning frown appearing.

'Yana and I were together for years,' he said, needing to help her understand. 'She'd always wanted children—we both did—so when we became engaged we thought it be best I get tested. I'd always known I could be sterile but I needed to be sure before we made that final commitment.' He shook his head, remembering how the results had knocked him sideways.

While he had always known he *could* be sterile, he'd never truly believed that he was. He'd come out the other end of treatment physically unscathed, so how could life throw him this at so late a turn?

It was as if fate had turned around and stuck a fork in him for daring to hope he could have a future with a family of his own.

'For two years I watched her suffer and turn into a shell of herself.' His voice had become hoarse. 'I would cringe to hear about any of her friends and family becoming pregnant, knowing it was another knife in her heart. But I thought I should be enough for her, that her yearning for a baby was something she should just forget about for my sake.'

'Couldn't you have adopted?'

'That's what Yana suggested, but I'm afraid adoption is not a route I will go down.'

'Your father adopted you,' she pointed out softly.

'And wasn't I made to know it? Hardly a day went by when Marat didn't rub my nose in the fact that he shared Andrei's blood and I didn't, that I was the cuckoo in the Plushenko nest. Andrei himself used the fact of Marat being his blood to undermine my point of view about bringing him onto the board at Plushenko's.' He raised his shoulders. 'I can't do that to a child. I won't see another person suffer for their blood not being the same as the family they live with.'

'How ridiculous.'

Whatever reaction he'd expected from Emily, scorn most definitely was not it.

'You don't know what you're talking about,' he refuted tightly.

'Rubbish. You have your mother's blood for a start—'

'Which meant nothing to her when she took Andrei and Marat's side.'

'You put her in an impossible situation. What was she supposed to do? Tell you that your ir-rationality was justified? I don't care what your father said, I'm certain he never meant it in the way you took it. He worked his fingers to the bone to keep you alive. If that isn't love then I don't know what is. For goodness' sake, he even got his hands on black market copies of *Top Cat* for you to watch when you were too weak to do anything else. Blood doesn't come into it.'

Her words were like tiny barbs being thrown at his skin, all landing straight in his chest. It took all his control to stop his hands from shaking.

He'd always been able to temper his anger but now...now he could feel it slipping.

She'd done this to him. He didn't know how or why but Emily pushed buttons in him that no one else could even find.

'You think because we've made love that you have a right to tell me how I should *feel*, is that it?'

'I never said that. There are thousands—millions, for all I know—of orphaned children in this world begging for a family to love them, and you won't consider taking one of them in and building a family of your own because of Marat's jealous attitude towards you.'

'You do not know what you're talking about.'

'Then explain it to me.'

'I don't have to explain anything to you.' He stared down at her. She gazed right back, her eyes full of hurt, but also full of a powerful anger. 'I've explained this much because after everything we've been through over these past few days I thought I owed you an explanation. I can't give a woman a baby and I will not be party to an adoption. Eventually, resentment rears its head and snap—' he snapped his fingers for emphasis '—the end of the relationship follows along with the mourning for wasted years. I couldn't give Yana the baby she wanted but in my arrogance I thought my love would be enough for her. It wasn't. She turned into a shell of herself and I won't—I can't—do that to you too. I won't watch the light in your eyes die.'

All the anger emanating from Emily's pores dissipated. She tilted her head, shaking it slowly. 'If Yana *had* loved you enough then you really *would* have been enough. Yes, I want children, but if I fell head over heels in love with someone who couldn't have them I would cherish the relationship for what it could give me and not what it couldn't.'

'You mean you would do what you have always done and stifle your desires for someone else's sake,' he said, unable to keep the bitterness from his voice.

'I feel sorry for you,' she surprised him by saying. 'Love isn't a tick-box or a competition.

I *know* I need to reclaim my life for myself but I will always be there for the people I love. I've let my father's depression and the way it affects me take over my life, always feeling I wasn't enough. I need to stop thinking like that and remember the good times with him, because when he's well our relationship is great.

'*That's* what I meant about cherishing a relationship for what it could give me rather than what it could not. And if I loved you, Pascha Virshilas, I wouldn't care about your sterility so long as you loved me back, and so long as I knew you would always be there for me.'

'But that's you all over, isn't it, *milaya moya*? And it's that life and passion you contain within yourself that lets me know I am right about this. I would not wish for all that life to die out. You deserve to have it all.'

'But not with you,' she finished for him softly.

'No. Not with me. I can't give you it all. All I can give you is unfulfilled dreams that will eventually eat into your soul and destroy you.'

'Then I guess there's nothing else for us to say,' she said quietly. Reaching up, she pressed a chaste kiss to his cheek. 'I hope one day you can look in the mirror and see a man who deserves to have it all too.'

CHAPTER THIRTEEN

EMILY HEARD THE front door open.

She took a sip of her lukewarm coffee and pushed her plate of half-eaten chicken pie to one side. She wasn't hungry.

She'd hoped with all her heart that her father getting out of bed was the first step towards recovery. But her return had set him back.

She'd returned to the house late last night, so had waited until the morning to give him the good news about the money and relay everything else Pascha had said. There had been no reaction, not even when she'd told him his job was there for him to go back to if he wanted.

He'd spent the day in bed.

She'd spent the day making phone calls and waiting for James to get back from work. It wasn't as if she had a job to go to. As she'd suspected, Hugo had fired her. The letter had sat on the sideboard waiting for her return. No severance pay. Nothing. She kept waiting for the devastation to hit her but, to her surprise, all she felt was relief.

It felt good to feel something. The only other emotion she felt at that moment wasn't even an emotion. It was numbness. She felt empty, as if she'd been drained of all the things that made her human.

'Hi, sis,' James said, stepping into the kitchen and heading straight to the oven where his dinner was keeping warm. 'Good trip away?'

'It was very…productive.' He didn't know about her job situation. Not yet. He could wait a little longer.

'Right. Well, I've rebooked my trip to Amsterdam and I'll be leaving on Friday.'

'When are you going back home?'

'After I've eaten this.' He winked at her, taking the seat opposite her at the kitchen table. 'I've missed my flat.'

'Funnily enough, I've missed mine too.' Emily waited for him to swallow his first mouthful. 'I've been thinking.'

'Did it hurt?'

For once she didn't laugh at her brother's quip.

'This can't go on. We can't fix Dad on our own—no, *I* can't fix him on *my* own. He needs professional help and he needs it now. I've phoned the doctor to get the ball rolling about getting proper home care for him.'

James eyed her shrewdly. 'What's brought the big change on? I thought you were adamant we didn't need outside involvement.'

'I was wrong. And I was wrong to give up my flat. I've given my tenants their month's notice. I'll be moving back in as soon as they're out. From now on, you and I are going to share responsibility for Dad.'

She didn't wait for a reaction, simply got up and reached for a shelf stacked with her mum's old cookbooks. She pulled one down and lobbed it on the table next to him.

'What's this?' he asked suspiciously.

'That, darling brother, is a sign from your little sister that it's time to grow up and learn to take care of yourself. Oh, and seeing as I cooked dinner, you can do the clearing up.' This time it was Emily's turn to flash a wink before heading out of the kitchen and up the stairs.

When she reached the landing, she took a deep breath.

That had been easier than she'd anticipated. There was definitely something to be said for not giving the other person time to answer back.

She heard the creak of her father's door and turned to find him standing at the threshold in his pyjamas, his eyes watery.

'There's something I need to tell you,' he said. And just like that, her slightly lighter mood plummeted.

Pascha sat in the back of his Lexus gazing absently out of the window.

It had all gone to hell.

Everything.

His driver turned the corner onto the road that housed his London office. A flash of curly black hair made him do a double-take.

Craning his neck for a better look, he soon realised the Monday morning street was so thick with bodies he must have imagined it.

He'd imagined he'd seen her a handful of times that day already. And a dozen the day before, when he hadn't even left his house.

If he was to see her now, in the flesh, he didn't know how he would react.

They pulled up outside his building and he got out, heading inside.

As usual, he was greeted by a bustle of activity. Normally he enjoyed the vibrancy and energy. Today he could do without it.

Today he wanted to be alone.

He didn't know what had propelled him to leave St. Petersburg late on Friday evening and come to London. After his confrontation with Marat, he could have gone anywhere. Why here?

Ignoring all the welcoming although still nervous smiles, he went straight up to his office. As he punched in the code to his office floor, he remembered he still hadn't changed it since Emily had sneaked in.

Cathy, the executive secretary he'd inherited when he'd bought Bamber Cosmetics, was there to greet him. His PA must have warned her to expect him.

'Can I make you a coffee?' she asked once the pleasantries were out of the way.

'No. I don't want any visitors or calls today either.' He swept into his office, closing the door firmly behind him.

The morning dragged.

He'd spent the weekend in his London home doing nothing but going over the events of the preceding week in his mind, which had culminated in his disastrous encounter with Marat.

He rubbed at his eyes with his palms and got to his feet. He needed to find some energy. Regardless of what had happened with Marat, he still had a business to run. More coffee should do the trick.

In his private room he switched the coffee machine on and read an email from Zlatan.

He was about to pour his coffee out when movement on the monitor caught his attention.

He stared. And stared some more.

No. He wasn't seeing things. There really was someone in his office. A pixie with a cascade of curly black hair.

Eyes fixed on the monitor, he took long, deep breaths and swallowed away the enormous lump that had formed in his throat.

Only when his composure was assured did he

pour his coffee out and step through the door to her.

'You seem to be making a habit of breaking into my office,' he said, striding over to his desk.

Emily was sat on the visitor's seat. As he passed her he caught a waft of her earthy honey scent. He tightened his grip on his cup, glad to place it on his desk as he took his seat.

Finally he could look at her properly.

What he saw made his heart wrench and his stomach dip.

She looked dreadful— really dreadful. Her skin was pale, her eyes red-raw, her hair even wilder than usual. She wore a deep-red jersey dress and thick black tights, her arms wrapped tightly around her waist as if for warmth or protection.

'I'm sorry for having to break back in,' she said, speaking tentatively.

'Evidently not sorry enough or you wouldn't have pulled the same stunt twice,' he said icily.

She blanched. 'I needed to see you. I didn't want this conversation over the phone. Cathy let me know you'd come in. She said you weren't accepting visitors so I waited until she went on her lunch break before sneaking in.'

'You know Cathy?'

She nodded.

And, just like that, everything fell into place: Cathy was the mole. His own executive secretary had given Emily his schedule and the code for the floor.

And, as all the pieces of the jigsaw slotted together, Emily's face crumpled as she realised what she'd given away.

'Oh, please, please don't punish her. Please. She did it for my family. She's worked here as long as my dad has—years ago, she was his secretary. She was my mum's best friend and used to babysit me and James. Please don't sack her. It's my fault. She didn't want to tell me anything but I used emotional blackmail to get your movements and the code out of her.'

Pascha held up a hand to stop the torrent of words spilling from her lips.

He had too much to think about as it was; his brain was overloaded. 'I will think about Cathy later. Tell me why you're here.'

A fat tear rolled down her cheek. She let it fall all the way to her chin.

He would *not* react to it. He would not react to her.

She reached into her large handbag and pulled out an envelope which she handed to him.

Wordlessly, he opened it. Inside was a cheque made out to him for the sum of a quarter of a million pounds.

'What is this?'

Emily's chin wobbled, her lips trembling, her eyes filling. 'It's the money I blackmailed you into paying my father. His bank account was credited late last week. I couldn't figure how to return it. Pascha, I... My...'

He waited while she tried valiantly to compose herself, hating that he had to fist his hands to stop them reaching out to her.

'You...were right all along,' she finally dragged out, her words stark. 'My father stole the money.'

Emily was still having trouble digesting it. For the past few days she'd thought of little else. She'd been so certain her father was innocent—one-hundred per cent positive. Doubt had never entered her head.

It wasn't just her father's actions she was trying to comprehend, though. The magnitude of what *she'd* done had hit her too.

She'd broken the law. She'd wilfully broken into Pascha's office with the sole purpose of stealing his files…had been prepared to use blackmail to get what she wanted…and for what? Because she'd wanted to fix her father.

Because she wanted him to love her when he was in the darkness as well as the light.

She couldn't fix what was in his head any more than she could fix him if he broke his leg. It was time to accept that.

'I already knew your father had taken the money.'

That shook her. 'You did?'

'It took Zlatan five minutes to learn that the money trail led straight to an account held by Malcolm Richardson.' Something that looked like sympathy flickered in his cold eyes before he cast his gaze back down to the sheaths of paper spread out before him.

Why was he being so cold?

Why wouldn't he look at her?

'He gave the money to the hospice Mum spent her last days in.'

'That doesn't surprise me.'

'How long have you known?'

'Zlatan told me an hour before the beach party.'

'Why didn't you tell me?' she whispered. 'Why did you transfer all that money into his account when you knew he was guilty?'

'Your father is ill. I do not want the money back and I will not be pressing charges.' To compound his point, he picked up the cheque and ripped it into little pieces. 'Keep this money. Use it to pay for full-time nursing care until he's well enough to care for himself.'

'It's too much,' she whispered.

'As far as I'm concerned, this is the end of the subject.' He indicated the door. 'Go home and tell your father he has nothing to fear from me. I wish him nothing but the best.'

What was *wrong* with him?

There was something…unkempt about him. A barely contained anger she hadn't picked up on initially because she'd been too full of the need to purge herself of her guilt.

He picked up an expensive-looking pen and

made a mark on a sheet of paper. 'Emily, I have a full schedule.'

'Too full to spend ten minutes with me?'

'Yes. Please leave.' He picked up a folder and opened it.

Legs shaking, she stood.

He really was dismissing her. After everything they'd been through, he was dismissing her as if she were nothing but a lowly employee.

Something inside of her went *ping*, a rush of fury that fired out of her fingers and had her leaning over his desk to wrench the folder from his grasp and toss it in the air.

As it fell to the floor, dozens of pieces of paper fell from it, floating and landing around her.

'What the hell did you do that for?' he snarled, his face contorting.

'I had to do *something* to get your attention. You're acting as if I'm nothing to you, as if I'm some stranger who's parked herself in your office. You won't even look at me!'

'That's because looking at you…' Whatever he was going to say, he cut himself off, punching his desk with a roar.

Shock at his response rendered her mute. All

she could do was stare at the man she loved and watch the unprecedented fury flow from him like a torrent.

Something was badly wrong.

'Why are you still here?' He got to his feet. 'I told you to leave.'

'What is *wrong* with you? Did something go wrong with the Plushenko deal?'

It was the mention of the word 'Plushenko' that sent Pascha's fury erupting through his skin.

Because of Emily, he'd finally understood that family meant more than pride.

Because of Emily, he'd gone to his brother with the truth, believing that this time things could be different.

He'd lost it all. Any hope of redemption and forgiveness was gone.

He'd laid everything on the line, revealed that he was the face behind RG Holdings. Revealed his need to make amends for their father's memory. When he'd finished his speech, he'd extended a hand. 'So what do you say?' he'd said. 'Are you prepared to draw a line under the past?'

Marat had stared at his hand before his thin lips had formed into a sneer. He'd pushed his chair back and got to his feet. 'I told you two years ago that I wouldn't sell the business to you. I would rather it went to the dogs than fall into your hands.'

How had he ever allowed himself to think that this time things might be different?

There had been no point in prolonging the meeting. He knew Marat, knew the entrenched look in his eyes. Pascha's reasoning had been disregarded. To try any more would have been akin to trying to reason with a toddler. 'I'm sorry you feel that way. I wish you luck in finding another investor.'

He hadn't reached the door when Marat had pounced, pinning him to the wall. '*You*,' he'd spat. 'It was always about *you*. No money for anything, not even the basics, because it all went on keeping *you* alive, the cuckoo in the nest who didn't belong there.' He'd abruptly let go and stepped back, throwing his hands in the air. 'And look at you now—rich and handsome. All that chemotherapy didn't even stunt your growth. You got everything.' His eyes had glittered with malice. 'But you didn't get Plushenko's. And you never will.'

Pascha had held onto his temper by the skin of his teeth. He was almost a foot taller than his adopted brother and, with around ninety-five per cent more muscle mass, all it would have taken was one punch to floor him and curb his cruel mouth.

Instead, he'd straightened his tie, dusted his arms down and said, 'It was never about Plushenko's. It was about family. Goodbye, Marat.' He'd left the office, striding past the waiting room where the lawyers were holed up, through the foyer and out into the cold St. Petersburg air.

He felt it now, as raw as if he were still in that conference room with his brother.

'The Plushenko deal is dead. It's over.'

Ignoring the ashen pallor of Emily's skin, he kicked his chair back and stormed over to stand before her. 'Plushenko's was built from my father's sweat and my mother's tears and now it's *gone*. Marat's hell-bent on destroying our father's legacy and there's nothing I can do to stop him.'

'You told him the truth?' she asked, her voice a choked whisper.

'Yes, I told him the truth. He threw my offer back in my face.'

Marat hadn't wanted anything to do with the cuckoo in the nest.

Why had he ever been foolish enough to believe otherwise?

'You wonder why I can't bear to look at you? You have *everything*—a family who loves you. You made me believe I could have that too. You gave me hope that Marat would accept me. You made it sound so easy. It was all a lie, a big, damnable lie, and every time I look at your face all I see is what could have been!'

Because of Emily, and that strange alchemy she had spread over him that had re-awoken his desire for a family of his own, everything had blown up in his face.

The path to his mother's forgiveness had been detonated. And that was the worst part about it.

'I'm sorry it didn't work out the way you hoped it would,' Emily said, breathing heavily, her face no longer pale, angry colour staining her cheeks. 'But at least you can look at yourself in the mirror and say that you tried, that you fought for a relationship with Marat.'

'It's destroyed everything. What hope is there for my mother to believe in me now?'

'Oh, get over yourself and stop being so defeat-ist!' Her fury seemed to make her expand before his eyes. 'As if presenting her with the gift of Plushenko's would magically have made things better between you—it hardly worked when you bought an island in her name, did it? Give her the one thing she hasn't got—her son. *You.* If I can love a stubborn fool like you, then I'm damn sure your mother can as well. She is *not* Marat. If you allow your stupid pride to kill your future with her, you have no one to blame but yourself.'

Leaving him standing there, his head spinning, she turned on her heel, pushed the door open and strode out, her head held high.

She didn't look back.

The miniature castle Pascha's mother called home was a world away from the small, dark house he'd been raised in. No flickering lights, no heaters where the oil level was checked with an anxious look, always quickly disguised if her young son happened to be watching her.

If Plushenko's shares continued to drop and its revenue continued to plummet, this beautiful home, with its bright, spacious rooms and indoor swimming pool, in theory would have to be sold.

Whatever the outcome of this meeting with his mother, he would ensure this home remained hers. He would buy her a dozen homes if she let him.

He'd arrived unannounced but she hadn't looked surprised to see him at her door. She'd invited him in with hardly a murmur.

Sitting on the sofa in the immaculate living room while she fetched them refreshments, his eye was caught by a photo above the fireplace of his mother and Andrei's wedding day. Everything about them looked cheap, from their wedding clothes to the cut of their hair.

The love shining between them, though, was more valuable than any Plushenko diamond.

He rose as his mother came through the door carrying a tray of coffee and biscuits.

'You're looking well,' he said after she'd taken the seat across from him. There was nothing cheap about his mother these days. Her salt-and-pepper hair had been expertly coloured a pale blonde, her calloused hands smooth from regular manicures.

'Thank you,' she said, with a warmer smile than he'd been expecting. 'You're looking good yourself.'

After a few minutes of small talk while they caught up on each other's lives, she rose to sit beside him. She patted his thigh. 'I know about you trying to buy Plushenko's from Marat.'

He stiffened.

It was the first time his mother had touched him in three years, since slapping him on his face after Andrei's funeral.

And no wonder that she had. In his arrogance, he'd thought she would be happy with the return of her prodigal son, that the promise of an island in her name would be enough to wipe out five years of hurt.

'I also know Marat…declined your offer. But that was to be expected.' She gave a sad smile that didn't reach her eyes. 'That boy always did have a problem with you. He was jealous.'

'Jealous of what?'

'Jealous of Andrei's love for you. Angry that he had to share his father.'

Emily had said the same thing.

She'd also said not to allow his pride—his *stupid* pride—to kill his future with his mother.

It had taken him two long, dark weeks to see how right she was.

Pascha took a deep breath. 'I'm sorry for cutting you and Papa out of my life all those years ago. I'm sorry for changing my surname out of spite. I'm sorry for rejecting all of your and Papa's attempts to reconcile with me, and I'm sorry Papa died thinking I didn't love him.'

'He knew you loved him.' Her voice was sad. 'You were his little shadow. He used to laugh and say if you could fit in his pocket to be carried around then you would. He was so proud that you wanted to be involved in the jewellery business with him. He always said that, without your drive, Plushenko's would have stayed a little firm floating along keeping its head above water.'

She reached out a hand to cup his cheek. 'You're not the only one to have regrets, Pascha. Andrei had them too. He blamed himself for your leaving, for forcing Marat onto the board against your wishes. And I regret spurning you after the funeral—my only excuse is that I was grieving.

But I have no excuse for not reaching out to you since.' Her eyes flickered with emotion. 'I think you must have inherited your pride and stubbornness from me. You're my son and I love you. I've always loved you. Andrei loved you too.'

She must have caught something in his eyes, because she continued, 'What he said about Marat being his blood—he didn't mean it to be taken that that made Marat more important than you. He meant that Marat was *as* important— that you were *both* his sons. He couldn't choose between you. He never gave a thought that you were not of his blood—to him you were his son and he loved you as fiercely as if you were.'

Pascha swallowed away the lump that had formed in his throat.

Emily had been right. Again.

Of course she had.

Her words had echoed in his head for the past fortnight, smothering his thoughts until he'd hopped onto his jet and demanded he be taken to St. Petersburg.

Emily understood love. She gave it freely, without conditions...

'Has Marat spoken to you about this?' he asked.

'I rarely see him,' she said with a shrug. 'Since Andrei died he doesn't bother with me. It wasn't just you he didn't want in his life. He didn't want to share Andrei with anyone. With me, he was just more subtle in showing his dislike.'

Pascha sighed and leant his head back. Now he thought about it, he could never remember Marat displaying any affection to her. He was always polite and cordial but never affectionate. Never a son.

And never a brother.

'If Marat didn't tell you, how did you know I tried to buy the company off him?'

This time his mother's smile carried to her eyes. 'I will show you.'

She left the room for a few minutes, returning with a folded up piece of white paper. 'This arrived last week from England. It was sent by courier.' She laughed. 'I think the sender used some kind of Internet translation for her Russian.'

Her?

His heart thundering, Pascha took the letter from his mother's hand and opened it. He knew who the sender was before he even started reading.

Printed out from a computer, he saw what his mother had meant. Emily's sentences were all jumbled, a literal translation from English of what she had tried to say. But her meaning was clear. Her words were heartfelt. Her plea was transparent: for his mother to understand just how much her son loved her and how their estrangement was destroying him.

'This Emily, she must love you very much,' his mother said after he'd read the letter all the way through three times.

He inhaled deeply, trying to hold on to emotions that threatened to smother him more than his thoughts had.

'Does this mean there is a wedding to look forward to?' she asked hopefully.

He shook his head slowly before dropping it forward and cradling it in his hands.

After everything he'd said to her, the blame he'd unfairly heaped on her shoulders, Emily had done *this* for him?

It had been a fortnight since he'd seen her. A whole two weeks without a word.

He'd missed her, badly enough that some nights he couldn't breathe through the pain.

How quickly the world could turn and change everything.

In all his years he'd never met a woman like her. Someone full of life. Someone with such intense loyalty... And an infinite capacity to love, just as Andrei had had...

He'd spent two weeks torturing himself with thoughts about whether or not she really had said she loved him. Her words had been shouted out in anger, to make a point.

Now, for the first time, his heart dared believe...

'I need to go,' he said, gripping his mother's shoulders and kissing her cheeks. 'I love you.'

'I love you too.' She smiled. 'Maybe soon you can take me to this island you named after me?'

'I would like that,' he said.

'And maybe I'll be able to meet this Emily?'

He attempted a smile of his own. He failed. 'I'm going to try my hardest to make that happen.'

CHAPTER FOURTEEN

PASCHA COULDN'T REMEMBER the last time he'd been to a photo shoot. When he'd first started buying fashion brands, he'd been fascinated with every aspect, but the novelty had soon worn off. Photo shoots were the worst. He was more than happy to leave the experts to deal with the day-to-day matters. After all, what did he know about fashion? Regardless, he didn't buy companies to tear them apart. He bought them to make a profit. Some needed restructuring or, in the case of the luxury luggage company he'd bought three years ago, a new marketing strategy. A few simple changes and that particular company had seen a four-thousand per cent increase in turnover— in its first year. Now that company alone had an annual turnover of half a billion dollars.

As he stepped into the vast white room filled with bodies hanging around not doing much at all, a small man with a silly flat cap on his head looked at him. 'You're too late. You were supposed to be here eight hours ago. We got a replacement for you.'

Taken aback, Pascha said, 'You must have me confused with someone else.'

'Aren't you a model?'

'No.'

'Shame. You could make a fortune.' He winked at him.

Too exhausted to react, Pascha said, 'I'm here to see Emily Richardson. I was told she was here.'

'She's through that door,' the small man said, pointing at the far end of the room. 'She's fitting Tiana into the last dress, so keep it quick—some of us want to get home tonight.'

Nodding his thanks, Pascha strolled to the door, aware of jumbled whispers around him. Someone had recognised him.

He opened the door.

'Two minutes,' the figure on the floor said without looking up.

Emily knelt barefoot at the feet of a statuesque model he assumed must be Tiana, doing something— he couldn't see what—to the hemline of the dress she was wearing

'Hello, handsome,' the model said, her eyes glittering.

'I will wait,' he said, ignoring her and parking himself on the nearest uncomfortable chair. On a rational level, he knew the model was beautiful. On a base level, she barely registered.

It was Emily he was here for. Emily, who he could see was a million miles removed from the gothic vamp he had first met, dressed in a pair of silver leggings and a green-and-orange-striped top that fell to her knees. He would wait for her for ever if he had to.

Tiana squealed. 'Ow! Watch what you're doing, will you?'

'Sorry,' Emily said, pressing her thumb to Tiana's ankle where she'd just inadvertently stabbed her with a sewing needle.

Hearing that voice for the first time in two weeks and in such an unexpected place had shaken her with the force of a battering ram.

Too scared to turn around and look at the waiting figure, she forced her concentration on the job in hand. Except her hands were shaking.

She could feel his stare fixed upon her. How she didn't stab the model again, she would never know.

Only when she was done and she'd sent Tiana back into the studio for the last shoot did she take a deep breath and turn her head.

She tried to speak, give a greeting of some kind. Her tongue wouldn't move.

She hadn't believed she would ever see him again.

She'd told herself she never *wanted* to see him again, but deep down she'd known it to be a lie. She would never seek him out, though. She was not a dog; she would not beg for scraps. Ironically, it was Pascha who had shown her she was worth more than that.

'How are things, Emily?' he asked, breaking the ice.

She nodded vigorously and forced herself to speak. 'Good. Good. Thanks.'

'I'm pleased to hear it.'

There was something different about him. She couldn't place what it was but it was there all the same. His hair? It didn't look quite as well groomed as it usually did. And he could do with a shave. The only animation on his face was his eyes boring into hers.

Unable to bear the weight of his stare, she began packing her things away, waiting with her lungs only half-working for him to give his reason for being there. There had to be a reason.

Did he know what she'd done?

'Are you enjoying working for Gregorio?'

'It's fabulous,' she said, forcing an injection of enthusiasm into her voice. It really was fabulous—she was loving every minute of it; she could hardly believe she'd landed the job so quickly.

She'd left Pascha's office full of anger and anguish, but also full of resolve.

Pascha had made it perfectly clear on his yacht that they had no future. Their awful confrontation in his office had made her accept it.

She could either allow herself to fall apart—and she knew it would be easy to do that; too easy—or she could pick herself up and carry on. And the best way to carry on was through work.

So she'd gone straight to the House of Alexander and spoken to Hugo, who was already feeling guilty for sacking her. He'd offered her her job back. She'd thought about it for all of two seconds before shaking her head. Working for Hugo, as great as it had been and as much as she'd learned, had stifled her. Instead, she'd asked if he would write her a reference.

The next day, armed with her portfolio and a glowing recommendation, she'd hit the London fashion houses. By the time she'd returned home, her phone was ringing. The House of Gregorio wanted her to come in for 'a chat'. Two days later, she'd started her new job.

Gregorio had a much more collaborative approach to design than Hugo. He wanted to see his designers' ideas whether or not they fitted with his 'visions'.

Work had kept her sane.

She'd tried to push Pascha firmly from her mind. And she thought she'd succeeded.

Seeing him again, though, only went to prove that all she'd been doing was suppressing her emotions.

The constant numbness in her belly had evaporated, jumbled knots tightening in its place.

'How's your father doing?'

'Much better.' At least she could speak coherently. 'The medication he's on is finally working and we've got him proper home help. It's making all the difference.'

'And is James now pulling his weight?'

She actually smiled, only fleetingly, but a smile all the same. 'I don't give him any choice.'

'I'm pleased to hear it.'

Looking him straight in the eye, she said, 'It's down to you. And for that I thank you.'

'You *thank* me?'

She nodded. 'Our time together…it made me see how much of myself I've supressed over the years, always trying to mould myself into what I think other people need. Now I have the courage to just be me, and if I need help now I ask for it. I know I can't fix everyone on my own. At least, I'm trying…' Her voice lowered as she considered what she'd done just a week ago.

Still on her knees, Emily used her hands to sweep the scraps of thread and material littering the floor around her. All she could concentrate on was breathing, trying with all her might to control the acceleration of her heart.

She'd regretted sending the letter the minute it had left her hand and gone off with the courier.

'I know about the letter you sent to my mother.'

She paused and dipped her head, closing her eyes. 'I'm sorry,' she said hoarsely. 'I don't know what possessed me.'

'I do.'

She jerked to feel his warm hand on her wrist, opened her eyes to find him on his knees beside her.

He put his palm on her cheek. 'You did it because you couldn't *not* do it. You did it because you have so much love flowing in your veins that you can't bear to see someone you love suffer, even if that person isn't deserving of your love.'

The feel of his skin on hers was almost too much to bear. 'Please tell me I didn't make things worse.' It was the one thing that haunted her.

He shook his head. 'You couldn't have made them worse.'

'I just felt so guilty for suggesting you to speak to Marat—'

'That wasn't your fault,' he cut her off. 'You made a suggestion, that's all, and I'm sorry for ever blaming you. I was hurting and full of guilt and I lashed out at you.'

'But…'

Before she could say another word, he kissed her, a gentle pressure that sucked all the air from her lungs.

'But nothing,' he said, his breath hot on her cheek. '*I* made the choice to speak to Marat, knowing damn well what the outcome might be. The letter you sent to my mother made a difficult situation easier. She was prepared for me to turn up on her doorstep.'

'I should never have interfered.' She turned her face away, tried to break away from him.

Such was his strength that he pulled her down and onto his lap, holding her tightly to him as she tried to move away. 'You're not going anywhere.' His large hands stroked her back with a firm tenderness.

'I swore I was going to stop trying to fix people.'

'But I love that you try and fix them.'

She froze.

'It's how you're wired,' he said gently. 'When you love someone, it's with everything you have. And I understand it now, because I know there is nothing in this world I wouldn't do for you.'

She raised her head to look at him.

'I always thought love was finite, that people were born with a certain amount they could give. I believed Marat when he told me I was the cuckoo in the nest and that our father could never love me like he loved him. You've shown me how wrong I was. The love I have for you binds me more tightly to you than any drop of blood ever could.'

He traced a finger down her cheek. 'I would give my soul for you and I can't ever apologise enough for the way I spoke to you in my office. I swear on everything I have that I will never speak to you like that again.'

He meant it. She could see it in his eyes. 'You were in pain,' she whispered. 'That's why I wrote to your mother—because it hurt me to see it.'

'Yes, I was hurting, but I should never have taken it out on you.' He breathed in deeply, inhaling her scent. 'I was scared. I've spent so many years believing myself to be unworthy of love that I couldn't see past it. That letter you sent to my mother—I can't tell you how that made me feel, knowing you had done that for me. If I could capture that moment I would cherish it for ever.' Now his eyes burned into hers, searching.

'You said on my yacht that if you loved someone you would cherish them for what they could give you and not what they couldn't.'

'I love *you*, Pascha. Sterile or fertile, it makes no difference to me.'

'I know you do. If there's one thing you've taught me, it's that love is infinite. Andrei loved me, truly loved me. And if you and he can love this stubborn fool of a man then I know I can love a vulnerable child who's desperate for a home.'

Pascha couldn't hold himself back any more. He needed to kiss her. Properly. He crashed his lips onto hers, holding her so tightly, kissing her so thoroughly, being so thoroughly kissed in return that all the tightness inside him loosened.

'Please, say you'll marry me? Will you become Emily Plushenko?'

'Of course I will…' That familiar groove formed in her brow. 'Emily *Plushenko*?'

He smiled sadly. 'I kept thinking of the butterfly tattoo in the small of your back and what a personal memorial to your mother it was. It made me think. If I can't restore Andrei's legacy, then I can honour him personally. I've changed my name back to Andrei's. I should never have turned away from it in the first place. But one thing I don't want to change is *you*. I love you for who you are, exactly as you are.'

'And I love you exactly as you are too.'

Suddenly it dawned on him, *really* dawned on him, that this passionate, crazy, loyal woman loved him. She loved *him*. She belonged to him just as he belonged to her. The only thing that bound them together was love.

And as he smothered her mouth in a kiss full of all the emotion pouring out of him, he knew their love would last a lifetime.

EPILOGUE

EMILY STEPPED ONTO the soft white sand holding onto her father's arm, the minuscule grains slipping between her bare toes. In the distance by the lapping waves she could see the archway covered in frangipani where the registrar stood beside an obviously nervous Pascha. She almost burst into laughter to see him in his traditional morning suit but with his own feet bare too.

With her simple yet traditional white wedding dress designed by Gregorio himself blowing in the gentle breeze, she walked towards him. She had no power to contain her beaming smile.

The look in his eyes made the beam grow even stronger.

The entire staff of Aliana Island was standing close by, all dressed in their finest, happily mingling with her family, Pascha's glamorous mother—who took one look at her soon-to-be daughter-in-law and burst into tears—and their few closest friends. Cathy—who Pascha had kept on without even revealing that he knew the truth about her being the mole—had an enormous smile on her face.

The only thing that marred the occasion was the absence of her mother and his father. And Marat. They'd sent him an invitation despite knowing they would get no response. Her loving, determined fiancé would never give up on that relationship. Whether Marat liked it or not, Pascha saw him as his brother; the ties that bound Pascha to him were too strong to be severed. Emily hoped with all her heart that one day Marat would come to accept him. She didn't hold any great hope, but for Pascha's sake she wanted it to happen.

In the meantime, her family had accepted him into the fold as if he'd always been there. He'd even let her brother organise his stag do, something he'd privately admitted he didn't want but had gone along with because he could see how much it meant to James. To his surprise, he'd actually enjoyed it, and now he and James were as thick as thieves, enough that Pascha had asked him to be his best man.

Best of all, they were going to create a family of their own. They'd already started the adoption process and were hopeful that, within a year, their home would be filled with the sound of a squealing child. Not one of them would be bound by blood, but they would all be bound by the one thing that mattered above all else. Love.

* * * * *

MILLS & BOON®
Large Print – May 2015

THE SECRET HIS MISTRESS CARRIED
Lynne Graham

NINE MONTHS TO REDEEM HIM
Jennie Lucas

FONSECA'S FURY
Abby Green

THE RUSSIAN'S ULTIMATUM
Michelle Smart

TO SIN WITH THE TYCOON
Cathy Williams

THE LAST HEIR OF MONTERRATO
Andie Brock

INHERITED BY HER ENEMY
Sara Craven

TAMING THE FRENCH TYCOON
Rebecca Winters

HIS VERY CONVENIENT BRIDE
Sophie Pembroke

THE HEIR'S UNEXPECTED RETURN
Jackie Braun

THE PRINCE SHE NEVER FORGOT
Scarlet Wilson

0415 Rom LP

MILLS & BOON®
Large Print – June 2015

MILLS & BOON®

Why shop at millsandboon.co.uk?

Each year, thousands of romance readers find their perfect read at millsandboon.co.uk. That's because we're passionate about bringing you the very best romantic fiction. Here are some of the advantages of shopping at www.millsandboon.co.uk:

* **Get new books first**—you'll be able to buy your favourite books one month before they hit the shops

* **Get exclusive discounts**—you'll also be able to buy our specially created monthly collections, with up to 50% off the RRP

* **Find your favourite authors**—latest news, interviews and new releases for all your favourite authors and series on our website, plus ideas for what to try next

* **Join in**—once you've bought your favourite books, don't forget to register with us to rate, review and join in the discussions

Visit **www.millsandboon.co.uk**
for all this and more today!